From the Case Files of Shelby Woo

THE CRIME: A break-in at a hip art gallery owned by Cindi's Uncle Phil threatens to bankrupt Phil and force his gallery to close.

THE QUESTION: Was someone looking to steal Cindi's prize photo—or destroy Uncle Phil's business?

THE SUSPECTS: *Janis Pine*—the owner of the gift shop next door thinks the "disruptive" kids hanging out at Phil's are scaring business away from her shop.
Dr. Halsey Taylor—the prominent veterinarian and art collector was seen arguing with Phil over the price of a painting. He feels Phil is trying to rip him off.
Gerald Vincent—Phil's landlord has been trying to oust Phil from the building so he can rent the space to a frozen-yogurt place.

COMPLICATIONS: Shelby courts danger as she tracks a wily culprit who's willing to do *anything* to keep her from discovering the truth!

The Mystery Files of Shelby Woo™

Available from MINSTREL Books

A SLASH IN THE NIGHT

ALAN GOODMAN

A
MINSTREL®
BOOK

Published by POCKET BOOKS
New York   London   Toronto   Sydney   Tokyo   Singapore

This book is a work of fiction. Names, characters, places and incidents are products of the author's imagination or are used fictitiously. Any resemblance to actual events or locales or persons, living or dead, is entirely coincidental.

A MINSTREL PAPERBACK *Original*

 A Minstrel Book published by
POCKET BOOKS, a division of Simon & Schuster Inc.
1230 Avenue of the Americas, New York, NY 10020

Copyright © 1997 by Viacom International Inc. All rights reserved.
Based on the Nickelodeon series entitled
"The Mystery Files of Shelby Woo"

All rights reserved, including the right to reproduce
this book or portions thereof in any form whatsoever.
For information address Pocket Books, 1230 Avenue
of the Americas, New York, NY 10020

ISBN: 0-671-01153-7

First Minstrel Books printing July 1997

10 9 8 7 6 5 4 3 2

NICKELODEON, The Mystery Files of Shelby Woo and all related titles, logos, and characters are trademarks of Viacom International Inc.

A MINSTREL BOOK and colophon are registered trademarks of Simon & Schuster Inc.

Cover photography by Jeffery Salter and Tom Hurst

Printed in the U.S.A.

For all the women in my life whose bravery, curiosity, strength, and creativity Shelby shares: my mom, Grace; sisters Leba and Marsha; my wife, Elena, and her mom, Lilliana . . .

and my Lily.

Chapter
1

Okay, this is driving me crazy. I've looked through everything Detective Hineline owns and I just can't find the copy of that speech he's supposed to give tonight on business security at the Cocoa Beach Business Boosters Club.

See, I work for the detective at the police station. And he was already home, ironing his shirt for tonight, when he suddenly remembered I forgot to give the speech to him when he left. My grandfather's bed-and-breakfast (that's where I live) is a lot closer to the police station than his house, so he thought maybe I could come over to the station and search, and he could just drive by and grab the speech through his car window on the way to the meeting.

But I've come up blank. I didn't leave it in the pile in his in-box, or in the pile in his out-box, or in his files under "B" for "Business," under "L" for "Locks," or even under "S" for "Security," or anywhere I can see.

And it's not in the top drawer, which is filled with pens and gum and junk, or in the drawer with all the blank arrest forms and complaint forms, or in the bottom drawer, where he keeps his gym shoes. Yuk!

I can't even call him. The detective must have left the phone off the hook after calling me, because I keep getting a busy signal.

Detective Hineline's always telling me I don't see things right in front of my nose. He says I miss obvious clues and jeopardize cases. But I've solved my share of mysteries around here lately, even if I don't ever seem to get credit for it.

In fact, just a few weeks ago, I solved a really tough mystery where the clues were anything but obvious. Think you're up to cracking it?

Let me get the casefile up on my computer.

A Slash in the Night

While I search for the detective's speech, see
if you can solve the case I call "A Slash in
the Night."

"Cindi, you're going to get us killed!" yelled
Noah, jumping onto the sidewalk as a car missed
him by inches. "And what's worse, you're hurt-
ing my arm!"

Noah Allen and Shelby Woo dashed through
the rain behind their friend Cindi Ornette, who
was not about to let heavy weather or traffic
stand in her way.

"We've got to get to Uncle Phil's gallery for
the Grand Opening!" Cindi said impatiently.
"Just stick with me, and you'll be perfectly safe.

"Hey!" she suddenly hollered at a driver cutting them off. "Are you nuts? Watch where
you're going!"

Shelby's eyes darted up to the thick black
clouds exploding with noise and water over their
heads. She hoped for a break in the violent
storm, but saw nothing but gloom in the sky
above them.

Noah glanced back at the Creamy Freeze just
up from the beach. He sighed. Just a few moments ago, he had been standing under the aw-

ning, dry, safe, and happily licking a double pistachio cone. The three friends were drenched, and so was Noah's ice cream, which he tried in vain to shield with the arm Cindi tugged.

"I don't get what the big deal is," Noah said, his left foot sinking into a water-filled pothole. "Why do we have to be there the minute he unlocks the door? So it's the 'Grand Opening.' Won't it still be open tomorrow? When clear skies are predicted?"

Shelby smiled. She was beginning to think Noah looked for opportunities to drive Cindi crazy. Noah knew why this event was important to Cindi. For the first time ever, one of her photographs was on display at her uncle's gallery, the Horizon Art Center. Ever since Noah and Cindi got their after-school jobs at Wavelength One-Hour Photo, she talked about nothing but being a professional photographer some day.

In fact, to celebrate the occasion, Cindi was all decked out in one of the fanciest outfits she had ever pulled together—a black velvet jacket over her father's old tuxedo shirt, which was cropped above her belly button; boy's burgundy satin pajama bottoms; and her red-and-black saddle oxfords with the platform heels. Even dripping wet, Cindi pulled it off.

Looking at Cindi sloshing through the rain, Shelby believed her friend's dream just might come true. This might be the beginning of a career shooting wildlife, famous celebrities, or important world leaders.

Shelby studied Noah, wondering about him. All Noah wanted to do was become an actor. Would he reach his goal?

And what about Shelby herself? Everyone assumed she would be a detective someday. Shelby wasn't sure that's what she wanted, but there was one thing she knew for certain. She loved solving mysteries.

"So, which photograph is it, anyway?" Noah asked, wiping raindrops from his eyes.

"Remember that day on the beach last spring," Cindi answered, "when it was unusually warm, and the foam from the water kept washing up over the pebbles and the sand?"

"Oh yeah, that day," Noah said sarcastically. "This is Cocoa Beach. Doesn't that happen *every* day?"

"No, no, no, this one day I had my camera. And I captured the landscape in detail. Just water, sand, and gravel. A study in textures and tones," she went on.

Noah eyed his ice cream, about to lose its balance on the cone, and tilted his wrist to compensate. "See, that's where you and I go our separate ways. I have a problem with the whole idea of landscapes. I like pictures with people in them," he told her. "Now, you take that picture of yours with the beach? Stick a volleyball game in there, cute girls in bathing suits on both teams, and you've got yourself some picture."

Cindi gave his arm a sharp tug. The jolt sent Noah's ice cream into the gutter.

"Hey!" he cried. "Look what you did, Cindi!"

"Noah, it's just ice cream," said Shelby. "And Cindi paid for it, to get you to come with us. After we see the show, you can get some more."

"Oh yeah?" he sputtered, watching the green lump bob along the narrow, sandy river toward the ocean, where the storm sewer emptied. "That ice cream is headed straight into the Atlantic. What if whales are lactose-intolerant?"

Shelby was about to laugh, but something she saw across the street made the laugh catch in her throat.

The three friends were facing the gallery. In

a small, single-story building on South Atlantic Avenue, it had two entrances. One opened into the main room, where Phil was building up a collection of paintings.

The other doorway led to a spare room Phil used as a teen center and exhibition space for amateur artists. That's where Cindi's photo was to be displayed.

And it was the condition of this door that instantly told Shelby something was wrong. The door hung at an odd angle, and the base of it was wedged against the sidewalk. The metal frame itself seemed twisted, like the door had been forced open.

Noah picked up on the peculiarity, too. "Is your uncle remodeling?" he asked Cindi as they entered.

But Cindi appeared not to hear him. "Wait until you see this picture," she bragged. "I helped Uncle Phil hang it just yesterday, so it would be ready for the official opening today. Did I tell you how I shot it? I was on the beach before sunrise and stood for hours, waiting for the light to be just right, so I could capture the scene in all its vibrant color and rich detail. Then

7

I set the focus and the exposure, took a breath, put my finger on the shutter and went *click*—''

At that moment, the three friends stopped in front of the picture frame on the wall where Cindi's photo was on display. They couldn't believe their eyes. All that remained was the photograph's jagged border, cut from inside its now-empty frame. Cindi's photo was gone!

Chapter 2

"My photograph!" Cindi cried.

Noah looked at the frame. "I don't know much about art," he offered, "but for me, this misses." Shelby elbowed him to be quiet.

Just then, Cindi's uncle walked up to them. "I'm sorry, Cindi. I can't believe this happened," he said, stroking his cat, Amber. "When I got here this morning, I found the break-in."

"Uncle Phil, this is awful. Did they steal your money or any of the valuable paintings?" Cindi asked.

The answer came from the other room.

"That's the strange part," said Detective Hineline as he walked up to the group.

"Detective," said Shelby, surprised to see him. She was his intern at the Cocoa Beach Police Department. He was never too happy to see her at the scene of a crime, even if she had a perfectly reasonable excuse for being there, like she did on this occasion.

The detective nodded at Shelby and the other kids, then turned to Phil. "I was kind of hoping we'd get some clue about the reports we keep hearing of stolen artwork being sold somewhere in Cocoa Beach," the detective said. "But whoever stole Cindi's picture left the valuable stuff."

Shelby thought about what the detective said. The area had a number of deep seaports that could be used by smugglers. She remembered the department frequently got bulletins about stolen artwork from all over the world, but nothing ever surfaced.

Shelby felt a flurry of emotions. On the one hand, she was sad for Cindi, whose artwork had been stolen. And she was angry for Cindi's uncle, whose door was smashed and business violated. But she couldn't deny the rush of excitement that crept up her spine.

Here was a mystery, right in front of her nose! Shelby stepped closer to the picture frame and examined it. Fingerprint dust covered the surface, left over from the crime specialists' examination of the slashed artwork. From the looks of things, the officers couldn't get any prints that could identify the thief.

Detective Hineline's face moved into Shelby's line of vision. "Excuse me, Shelby, am I in your way?" he asked her sarcastically.

She took a step back and looked up at the detective, embarrassed to be caught investigating at his crime scene.

"Shelby, you won't find anything we missed," the detective insisted. "There weren't any fingerprints on the frame itself, and none on the door handle where the thief broke in. Nothing else in the gallery was touched. No muddy footprints were found on the floor. The prowler didn't drop any handkerchiefs or tools. Outside, there aren't any incriminating tire treads, candy wrappers, or signed statements saying, 'I did it.'

"And the fact that all the really valuable art was left alone, and just Cindi's picture was taken, tells me this had to be the work of an amateur. I'm sorry, Cindi," the detective concluded, realizing he may have insulted Shelby's friend.

But Cindi just stared at the empty frame, lost in thought.

"I'm not sorry," she blurted out. "Don't you see what this means? Someone really wanted my photograph. It was the only thing taken. Somebody must think I really have talent!"

That was just like Cindi, Shelby reflected. Most people would be upset about their artwork being stolen. Cindi got excited that someone wanted it.

She started talking about other photos she had shot and what they might be worth. "Remember those pictures I took of the big rocks at the base of the Cocoa Beach pier? You think they might be valuable?"

"Sure," said Noah. "If people are stealing photos of a beach, rocks should cause a riot."

Cindi grabbed his empty ice cream cone and shoved it into his mouth. "Don't talk with your mouth full," she replied.

With nothing more to do at the crime scene, Detective Hineline left to file his report, telling Phil he could open the gallery and let in the customers.

Phil walked past the front desk and bulletin board where he left messages for himself, and went to open the main entrance, where a customer was waiting for him. Shelby and her friends could hear the conversation with the customer through the connecting doorway to the teen center.

"Dr. Taylor," Phil said, greeting the man. Shelby recognized Dr. Halsey Taylor, a local veterinarian. His office in town was small, but he owned a large, modern home right on the beach near Fisherman's Wharf.

Very tall and slender, with a thin mustache resting right on top of his thick upper lip, Dr. Taylor smiled through teeth as broken, twisted, and discolored as a rotting picket fence. His grin made Shelby extremely nervous, but apparently dogs and cats found it comforting, she assured herself.

"And how's our friend Amber?" the doctor asked, looking at the cat in Phil's arms.

"Fine, since the last time you saw her," Phil answered. "But feistier since her accident."

The doctor nodded, then walked directly over to a canvas. He stood very straight in front of it, with his hands behind his back. Rocking back and forth on his heels, his eyes never strayed from the work he was admiring, an abstract painting of a chair.

"You came to look again at the Dorot?" asked Cindi's uncle, referring to Guillaume Dorot, whose name was scrawled along the bottom of the canvas.

"Yes," said the doctor, "to admire, and perhaps, to buy. That is, if we can finally agree on a price."

"It's a pleasure to know someone else who appreciates it," said Phil, "but we've discussed this before, Dr. Taylor, and you know how I feel."

He pointed around the gallery to the other paintings, and continued. "Everything else you see in the gallery, we sell on behalf of the artists, and receive a commission for the sale. But this"—he pointed to the painting of the chair—"is the only piece of art of any real value that I actually own, and it isn't for sale."

Shelby saw the doctor's smile disappear. His eyes flashed once around the gallery. "You are building a nice collection," he told Phil. "But the Dorot is all I want."

His eyes shifted toward the teen center, where Shelby and her friends stood. Shelby turned her back, not wanting to appear to be eavesdropping on the conversation. "Trouble today?" the doctor asked.

"A break-in," Phil answered. He looked back at Cindi. "And the thief got one of my favorite pieces, too, by an undiscovered local photographer, someone I think is going to be a major talent someday."

Shelby looked at Cindi. She saw her friend's face flush with pride.

"Well then, that's not too bad, is it?" Dr. Taylor replied. Then he turned to Phil and spoke quietly. "I've been a loyal customer, Mr. Ornette. But if you won't sell me your best work, you've sold me the last painting I'll buy from you. You won't see me again until they slam the doors on this place for good, and you have to auction off your precious art to save your shirt!"

Dr. Taylor walked so briskly toward the gallery exit that Cindi's uncle had to brush past the doctor to block the door. He stuck out his right hand.

"I'm sorry this has gotten unpleasant," Phil told the doctor. "We've always gotten along in the past, and you've been a good customer. I hope we can do business again in the future."

Dr. Taylor looked down at Phil's hand, but

didn't meet it with his own. Instead, he pushed past the gallery owner and out the door into the Cocoa Beach street. He turned his collar up against the rain and walked across the intersection.

"Whoa," said Shelby as Cindi's uncle rejoined the kids in the teen center, "what a creep."

Noah agreed with her about the rude customer. "Yeah. And so upset over a painting of a chair. There isn't even anybody sitting in it."

"Want us to stay and help you clean up?" Cindi asked her uncle.

"No, that's okay, Wayne is coming later," he answered. Wayne was Cindi's cousin.

As the weather began to clear, the kids toured what remained of the exhibit. It included photographs like Cindi's that showed some of the more familiar spots in Cocoa Beach; paintings of rock stars, still lifes, and dream fantasies; other pieces that were simply vivid splashes of color; and a collage of trash salvaged from the beach that was a young artist's ecology statement—gum wrappers, handbills from local clubs, a torn sleeve from a baby's T-shirt, and a piece of plastic broken from a snorkel.

Before leaving, Phil insisted the kids sign his

Guest Book. When it was Shelby's turn, she bent to the desk with pen in hand and noticed the date on the top of the page—October 11.

On a hunch, she turned the book back one page to October 10. Her finger slid down the list of names she found there.

"Shelby," Cindi said. "You ready?"

"Huh? Oh, yeah, sure," Shelby answered. She turned the page over and signed her name.

"I liked the snorkel and trash thing," said Noah as the kids left the gallery.

"Why?" Cindi asked him.

Noah thought for a moment, then explained. "Thanks to that artist, who went and picked up all that stuff, next time I'm at the beach I won't step on any of it. Hey, should we check out C.J.'s?"

C.J.'s was a burger joint just a few doors up the street. "Didn't you just finish an ice cream cone?" Shelby teased him.

"Oh yeah," Noah answered, remembering his ice cream bobbing down the rain gutter, "that cone is definitely finished. What do you think, Cindi? C.J.'s for some fries?"

"I'm wondering what Shelby was looking for in the Guest Book," Cindi mused.

Shelby's eyes darted over to her friend. "I really have to get more subtle, don't I?"

"Spill it," Cindi demanded, her eyes growing wide.

Well, I remembered something you said when we were walking to the gallery. I thought it might provide a lead, maybe even my first clue toward solving the mystery of who stole your photograph.

"Wait until you see this picture," Cindi bragged. "I helped Uncle Phil hang it just yesterday, so it would be ready for the official opening today."

I think the person who stole your picture knew it was there. Look how deliberate the thief was, passing up all those other paintings and valuable works to get to it.

Noah jumped to the same conclusion: "And since the picture only went up yesterday, maybe the thief was one of yesterday's visitors," he reasoned.

18

"The signatures in the Guest Book!" Cindi cried. "Your first clue, Shelby!"

Noah chimed in. "Any names pop out at you?"

Shelby's eyes brightened. "One name," she said. "Dr. Halsey Taylor."

Cindi stopped right in the middle of the street and grabbed Shelby's arm. "That jerk was there yesterday after we hung the picture! He stole it!"

"Not necessarily," said Noah.

Cindi turned to him. "What do you mean? It's so obvious."

"Well, you're assuming the person who stole the picture signed in," Noah explained. "Not everybody does. I mean, I didn't."

Cindi thought about that a moment, but a car-horn blast sent them all flying to the opposite sidewalk.

"Noah's right," Shelby said when they were safely on the other side. "There could be other people who were there that we don't know about. But the veterinarian is definitely a suspect."

"Maybe when he gets out of prison, he'll want to start collecting my photographs," Cindi said hopefully.

Shelby smiled. You couldn't keep that girl down long. Looking up, Shelby saw the familiar front door of C.J.'s, a natural gathering place for local kids in Cocoa Beach.

"You know, I've got to get going," Shelby said. "I promised my grandpa I'd gather the sheets and towels for the laundry truck that picks up our stuff. But I'll talk to you guys later, okay?"

The friends said good-bye and went their separate ways.

The morning's excitement left Shelby with very little time to get home and deal with the laundry, but if she hurried, she could still get it out and do a little cleaning around the bed-and-breakfast inn before her grandfather got back from his dentist appointment.

Shelby turned and walked a couple of blocks away, squinting into the sun. In the early fall, the weather could be so unpredictable—pouring rain one minute, the harsh, white sun beating down without relief the next. But at least the ocean air made Cocoa Beach bearable in this season. The rest of Central Florida fried so badly in the sun, it was downright unlivable.

Deep in thought and squinting in the blinding

sun, Shelby rounded the corner and brushed by a small woman, old and frail, with a broad-brimmed straw hat.

It was just a slight, inadvertent bump. But a piercing scream cut through the air as if the woman had been mugged and beaten.

"Oops," said Shelby. "Are you all right?"

Instead of an answer, the woman screamed again. Then she raised her umbrella high over her head, ready to strike Shelby!

Chapter
3

Shelby shielded herself with her arms, protecting her face from the woman's umbrella.

"Why don't you look where you're going?" the woman demanded in a strong voice.

"I said I was sorry," Shelby answered, trying to focus her eyes. "It was the sun. I didn't see you."

Shelby stood there another moment or two, peeking out through her arms, trying to make the blurry image in front of her gel into a woman's face. The broad-brimmed hat prevented her from getting a good look.

"Well, you gonna move? I'd like to get out of this sun sometime today," the old lady barked at the girl.

Shelby apologized again, for all it mattered. Then she stepped aside to let the woman pass.

The commotion caused a stir on the street. Heads turned, and a few doors opened as shopkeepers looked toward the source of the scream. As the woman moved away, Shelby shrugged at the concerned faces, to let them know everything was okay and that she was as puzzled by the outburst as they were.

You meet all kinds in Cocoa Beach, Shelby thought. She couldn't tell whether the woman was a local or a tourist. But she hoped to never run into her again.

Still shielding her eyes from the sun, Shelby glanced at the digital clock in the window of the bank. The laundry truck would be arriving at the inn any second. She'd have to run. Taking big breaths as she jogged, she noticed the wonderful smell of clean and renewal after a thunderstorm.

Along the dirt road that led to her grandfather's bed-and-breakfast, the tree limbs hung thick with Spanish moss that broke the sunlight into choppy, kaleidoscopic patterns. Even with the dirt road turned to mud, as it had after this morning's rain, Shelby loved to run through the neighborhood, glancing up at the gardens and porches of her neighbors.

The larger houses belonged to people who worked in one of the many businesses related to the aerospace industry. Others were the vacation retreats and retirement homes of people who had come to Cocoa Beach from all over the country. Shelby liked to imagine, as she passed each one, what their lives might be like, what secrets the people kept, what had brought them to this spot.

Kicking her heels up behind her, Shelby thought about her own life, and the strange circumstances of her coming to Cocoa Beach. Living with her grandfather had been a dream come true for her. A former crime specialist with the San Francisco police department, Mike Woo used to send letters to Shelby in China about the cases he helped solve in the police laboratory.

Maybe it was growing up in such a strict society that made his stories so fascinating to her. How strange, undisciplined, and unpredictable life in the United States seemed to her. The characters in his reports were like nothing she'd ever encountered.

Shelby would read and reread each adventure,

envisioning a day when she could solve mysteries, too. Her parents watched that interest grow and grow, and an idea hatched. Their hearts brimming with joy—knowing they were helping to fulfill their daughter's dream—and at the same time breaking with the sadness of sending her to the United States, her parents offered her the chance to live with her grandfather, by that time retired in Cocoa Beach.

Shelby had leaped at the chance.

It was easier then to say yes, not realizing as she did now, a few years older, how much she would miss her parents and how hard it would be for a young Chinese girl to adjust to the United States.

Shelby turned the corner at Vidalia Street and paused to catch her breath in front of a small community church, where young children played in the yard.

A red rubber ball rolled into the road and came to rest at Shelby's feet. She picked it up and aimed to toss it back into the yard. Running to the edge of the grass, a tiny Asian girl, no more than four years old, looked up at her with arms outstretched. Shelby smiled. The little girl broke into a wide grin in return.

With a gentle arc, Shelby lobbed the ball at the little girl, whose hands tried to catch it. The ball slipped between them and rolled away into the yard. Forgetting entirely about Shelby, the girl chased the ball back to her friends. Shelby took a few deep breaths and resumed her run.

Even though she had been older than the little girl at the day-care center when she came to the United States—almost thirteen—making friends wasn't easy for Shelby. She was usually the only Asian kid in her classes, and at times felt like such an outsider. Some kids made fun of her name and her accent.

Except for Cindi and Noah, of course. The first day they met, Cindi wanted to hear everything about her life, from Shelby's first minute of consciousness. She was intensely curious about this new girl sitting next to her in class.

And Noah, the actor, was such a brutal mimic of the kids who taunted Shelby. If someone said something mean, Noah would repeat it in a way that made the kid appear to be a total geek. He made Shelby laugh, and it took the sting out of the insult.

Adjusting to the different pace and standards took time, but a real plus was living at the bed-

and-breakfast, a large house her grandfather had purchased to earn income during his retirement. After all his years in the United States, Mike Woo still loved to tell stories about the old days, back in China, and his own first years in America. They shared traditional meals and conversation that warmed her heart.

Meanwhile, Grandpa Mike taught a few courses in crime science at the local college, and occasionally advised the police, just to keep his hand in the business. Whit Hineline was one detective he had helped on a case, and the detective returned the favor by getting Shelby her after-school job at the police station.

She also loved living at the Easterly Breeze for the excuse it provided to snoop on people. She tried not to get caught at it, but the constant stream of visitors to Cocoa Beach who stayed at their inn gave her the opportunity to conduct her own private research study on human behavior. Quiet couples with way too much luggage; loners who never left their rooms but made lots of long-distance phone calls; scientists working on top secret projects—each week brought new faces from Maine, Ohio, Texas, and Oklahoma.

But then there were the disadvantages—chores.

Her sneakers covered with mud, her lungs empty, Shelby rounded the corner and saw, in the distance, the laundry truck disappearing down the road.

"Hey! Hey, come back!" she screamed at the top of her lungs. She waved and jumped frantically, splashing mud up her leg. The truck accelerated, the driver unaware of her.

On her last jump, Shelby's right sneaker stayed lodged in the mud and her foot pulled out. Thrown off balance, her white sock landed in the brown ooze, and then she slipped and fell on hands and knees.

She picked her chin up and peered, panting, down the road as the laundry truck disappeared.

The sound of an engine behind her whipped her head around. Bearing down on her, splaying mud in all directions, was a car full of kids.

There was no time to get up out of the way. All Shelby could do was drop and roll.

She tumbled across her left arm and over on her back, barely slipping out of the way before the car's tire flattened her sneaker. The kids in the car never saw her.

Picking herself up, she retrieved her sneaker and trudged up the driveway to her home. She'd have no choice but to do the sheets and towels herself.

Shelby looked up. The clouds had cleared, and it was becoming a beautiful Saturday afternoon . . . a beautiful Saturday afternoon she'd spend in the basement, standing over the washing machine and dryer.

The weekend passed before she could see her friends Cindi and Noah again. The bed-and-breakfast was filled to capacity, and with just Shelby and her grandfather to take care of all the guests, she spent a busy Saturday and Sunday cleaning, helping with shopping and sightseeing recommendations, and assisting with checkout and luggage. Then there was homework, which was always a top priority with her grandfather, who watched over her.

At school on Monday, Cindi was still excited about the prospect of kick-starting her photography career, thanks to the notoriety provided by the gallery break-in. She told everyone about it, offering them a special portrait package.

"You know how the school pictures they take every year always look so doofy?" she asked one group of kids in the corridor. "Well, let's see if those guys can stand some competition from me."

There weren't any takers, but Cindi told herself that launching a new business always took some time. Most of the kids asked instead about the teen center, wanting to know if it was in any jeopardy. In the short time since Phil opened it to kids, it had already become a favorite place for after-school activities.

Wanting to learn herself if there had been any developments in the case, Shelby decided to stop by the gallery on her way to the police department after school. Noah and Cindi went with her.

The teen center entrance was still covered with plywood, so they entered through the gallery. Inside, they found Phil deep in conversation with a stocky man with black hair and round, black-framed glasses. He had the annoying habit of looking around the room while he talked, giving the impression he wanted to stay alert to anything that might be more interesting than the person talking to him. He never looked at the kids.

"I just need a little more time," Cindi's uncle

told him. "One good sale, and I'll have the money."

Shelby listened intently. It sounded like Phil was having financial problems, and was being pressured by the stout man.

"And I have a lease that says you pay me or you're out!" the man told him.

"Gerald Vincent," Cindi whispered to Shelby. "He's my Uncle Phil's landlord."

Shelby nodded slowly; she knew of him. He owned other properties around town, including the optimistically named Space Coast Speedway, which was actually a broken down go-cart track.

Phil spotted the kids and smiled, as if to tell them everything was fine. Shelby decided to take advantage of the opportunity to spend a little more time looking around the gallery for clues about the crime.

Inside the teen center, a small group of kids was already busy playing and talking about the latest CDs while they browsed through Phil's art books. Shelby walked to the spot where Cindi's photograph had hung. Could Cindi's photo have been the first piece the intruder saw, and the easiest to steal? And could that be why the thief selected it?

Checking her line of sight, Shelby realized Cindi's picture was all the way across the room, but in a little alcove along the side wall. It couldn't be seen from the door at all. Someone must have really wanted the picture to go straight for it.

"Meow," she heard from behind her. Amber was creeping along the wall, spying on the activity.

"What's wrong, Amber?" Shelby asked, bending to stroke the cat. "What happened here?"

Without warning, the cat hissed and struck Shelby, tearing across her wrist with its claws. Shelby pulled her hand back, and the pain made her cry out.

"Shelby!" Phil said, hearing her. Instantly he was at her side, examining the wound with Cindi and Noah. "Are you all right?" Phil asked. "Let me look."

"No, don't worry. She didn't even break the skin," Shelby told him, rubbing her wound. She held it up to show him the thin marks rising across her wrist.

Phil swooped down and gathered Amber up in his hands, then walked through the curtain into the office. Reappearing, he explained the cat's behavior. "Amber was hurt in an accident; she lost a claw in a fall and hasn't been too friendly since. I'm so sorry."

Shelby reassured him. "Really, I'm fine."

Phil rejoined his landlord. "Look, I might not have this month's rent right away," Phil told the man.

"Then it looks as though I'll have an empty building, won't I?" said Vincent, his head darting toward the door. "And I know just the frozen yogurt chain that would be happy to pay twice the rent."

Vincent strode quickly to the door, but Phil called to him. "Look, can't you help me out?" he asked.

"Sure," Vincent answered, thumbing through the paperwork on Phil's desk. Cindi watched him. His snooping into Phil's private things annoyed her. "I'll help you," he told the gallery owner. "I'll help you pack."

Phil was quiet after Vincent left. Cindi sensed something deeper was troubling him. "It's more than just the rent, isn't it, Uncle Phil?" she asked him.

Phil bit his lower lip and walked to the front desk. He held up a document.

"When the insurance agent came to look at the damaged door, instead of handing me a check, he gave me this," he told the kids.

Shelby looked at the paper more closely. It was stamped "CANCELLATION" in big block letters.

Shelby knew what that meant, because of the high insurance premiums her grandfather paid to keep the bed-and-breakfast secured. Losing its insurance could mean the end of the Horizon Art Center.

"How can they do that?" Noah asked. "One lousy break-in, and they cut you off?"

"Not exactly," Phil explained. "Three warnings and a 'last notice' letter, and they cut you off. When you don't pay them, that is."

Cindi sat down hard in a chair, stunned. "But Uncle Phil," she asked, "why didn't you pay them?"

"That's the thing I don't understand," he replied. "I did. At least, I thought I did."

He explained that the gallery was always short of cash, but selling a painting the previous week had provided the funds he needed to pay the bill. That's when he wrote the check to the insurance company.

"I distinctly remember putting it in the stack

of mail here on the front desk. It was the last check I wrote, the last one to go in an envelope and get sealed. I'm sure it went out with the other mail that day," he assured them. "There's no way I would have forgotten it. I had a note to myself tacked to the bulletin board all week to remind me it was due."

But the insurance company never received it, he told them. Not only wouldn't the company pay for the broken door, but because they now considered Phil's business to be a bad risk, Phil would be forced to pay a huge increase to have his policy reinstated.

"I showed them the check stub in my checkbook, but they wouldn't accept that as proof," Phil told them. "The agent was sympathetic, but said he couldn't do anything about it.

"Replacing the door won't be that much money," Phil continued, "but a business can't operate without insurance. So I used the money I should have paid to Vincent to renew my insurance policy. I just can't figure out what happened to that check. Lost in the mail, I guess."

Noticing how depressed the three were getting, Phil changed the subject. "You know, I don't want you kids to worry. Something will turn up, I'm sure."

Cindi spoke up. "But, Uncle Phil, there must be something we can do."

"Let me think about it," he told her. "But in the meantime, don't you kids have your jobs?"

He was right. Shelby was due at the police station, and Cindi and Noah had to get to the photo shop. Cindi touched her uncle's arm and gave him a sympathetic smile as she left the gallery.

There was time for a soda at C.J.'s before they were due at their jobs.

"What Uncle Phil should do is give me my own one-woman show," Shelby's best friend said. "You know, as a benefit for the gallery. I would turn over all the money from the photo sales to him. Can you imagine my pictures everywhere you look?"

Cindi pushed open the door to C.J.'s and practically skipped inside. . . .

Until the image in front of her face stopped her dead in her tracks.

There—tacked to the wall amid the knick-knacks and rubble, crumpled, with jagged edges and covered with stains—was Cindi's photo!

Chapter
4

"Well, mystery solved," Noah said, "except for one thing. Why would someone steal *that*?"

Cindi looked at him with cold eyes. "It's upside down," she told him. Walking over to the wall, Cindi pulled out the thumbtacks, spun the print, and reattached it, standing back to admire it.

Noah gazed at the righted image, covered with coffee grounds, ketchup drips, and mustard smears. "Oh, well, now I see it," he told her.

Shelby turned to Will Potter, the part-time counterman at C.J.'s and a friend from school. "Will, do you have any idea how this picture got here?" she asked him.

Will looked up from the grill. "Sure do," he answered. "I put it there, after I found it Saturday morning. But do me a favor and don't ask about the chili stains on the wall behind it. I plead ignorant on that."

Cindi turned to Will. "But there are stains all over my picture, too," she said.

The boy answered without looking up again. "Of course there are. Did you ever look at what we dump in the trash?"

This was almost too much for the young photographer. "Trash! You found my picture in the trash?"

Shelby sat at the counter, pondering. "This makes no sense," she said. "Why would someone break into Cindi's uncle's gallery, steal a picture right out of its frame, and dump it in the trash behind C.J.'s?"

Cindi refused to believe that was what happened. "This is a valuable piece of art," she told her friend. "Maybe the thief just—umm—lost it by accident? And it got picked up by someone else who didn't realize its value?"

Shelby could see Cindi was hurt that someone would unceremoniously toss something that made her so proud. She tried to think of a way to cheer her up.

"Don't you see—your photograph could be at the center of a real mystery," Shelby told her.

Cindi brightened a little. "You think so?" she asked. The girls went back to the wall for a closer look.

Meanwhile, Noah leaned over the counter. "So, here's a question," he began. "What were you doing digging in the trash?"

"Sometimes you find really cool stuff in there," Will answered.

"Uh-huh," Noah said. "Name one thing you ever found in the trash bin that's cool."

Will looked at Noah, puzzled. "Cindi's photo," said Will. "Haven't you been listening?"

Quickly, Shelby ran down the events of the past few days for Will and asked him if he was at the burger joint Friday night, the night the picture was stolen.

"Why?" Will asked. "Am I a suspect?"

"Not just now," Noah answered in a deep voice, "at least not regarding the stolen photo. But we may have to hold you in the chili-on-the-wall incident."

Will looked at the photo. He told Shelby he

wasn't working that night, but came in after a movie.

"Do you remember anything unusual?" Shelby asked.

"Well, yeah," Will answered. "And I wasn't the only one, either. Lots of people were complaining that the popcorn bags weren't as full as they used to be."

Shelby and her friends just stared at him. It could sometimes take a moment or two for Will to get the point. This was one of those times. Will scanned their faces. He squinted. Gradually, it dawned on him. One finger went up as he pursed his lips in realization.

"I'm gonna guess you meant, was there anything unusual here at—"

"Yes!" Shelby cut him off.

"Just the regulars. Mr. Rigsby from the laundry service, delivering clean towels and aprons and stuff," said Will. "He always sits and has coffee and pie."

"And . . ." Shelby prodded.

"Mr. Claiborne, the guy who owns that used-book store at the mall," Will answered. "He always asks for the special and drinks herb tea."

"Who else?" Shelby asked.

Will thought a moment, then answered. "Well, Janis Pine came in—she always does." He turned to Cindi. "She's that old lady who owns the tourist shop next door to your uncle's gallery."

"I've heard about her, but I've never been in her shop," Shelby said to Cindi.

"Me neither," said Cindi. "I wonder why? Maybe it's that giant sign on the door that says, 'No Kids Allowed!'"

"How warm and inviting," said Noah.

"She's always complaining to my uncle about the noise next door at the teen center. I peeked in her window once. The store is full of all these shelves with little bitty glass figures and trinkets," Cindi said. "Maybe she's afraid kids will bust up her stuff."

"What's she like, Will?" Noah asked.

"Every day for lunch, Janis Pine comes in for soup," Will answered. "After she closes the gift shop at night, she gets another cup to take home."

"No, I meant 'what's she like,' as in 'what is she like,' not 'what does she like to eat,'" Noah explained.

"Oh," Will said. "Well, she's—just normal, I guess."

"Oh yeah," said Noah. "I'd say that soup business is highly suspicious behavior." He looked around at the inquisitive stares from his friends, then said, "Have you ever tasted their soup?"

Shelby filed in her head the information about C.J.'s late-night visitors. "Will, let me know if you remember anything else?" she asked, about to leave.

"Sure," the boy answered her. "I can even mail it to you with this free stamp I found. If I can just get it off this empty envelope."

She took a step, but then his comment registered. Her head snapped around. Will was holding a small envelope with a window cut in the front, the type used for paying bills.

"Free stamp you found?" she repeated. "Where exactly did you—?"

He pointed a finger toward the back of the restaurant. "In the trash. Right next to the photo," he told Shelby.

"Will, can I see it?" Shelby asked, excitement in her voice.

Noah took the envelope, so he could hand it to Shelby. Then he wiped his hand on Will's apron.

Shelby examined the envelope and its stamp.

"If this is what I think it is . . ." she said as she moved to the door.

Cindi took a business card off the wall near the phone where it was tacked, turned it over, and set it down on the counter. She started to write something on the back. But Shelby was in too much of a hurry to ask what it was.

"Come on," she told her friends. "This envelope and stamp could be an important clue!"

Chapter
5

As Shelby raced back to the gallery with the stamp, she thought about Cindi's uncle and the work he had put into the business. She knew how difficult it had been for Phil. Running the art gallery was still something new for him.

He had been a local art teacher, one particularly liked by class after class of students at Space Coast High. Years of scrimping and saving had finally allowed him to quit the teaching job and open his own gallery space. However, starting the business nearly wiped out Phil's savings. And his son, Cindi's cousin, Wayne, needed a scholarship to attend college.

Business was slow at first, but there had been

a few notable sales, to customers such as Dr. Taylor. Even though the business was a strain on their finances, Phil's family supported his hunger to have a first-rate gallery with important works of art for sale.

With his new career far from secure, Phil still refused to abandon the kids he'd taught in the school's art program. The whole idea of the teen center was to encourage kids to appreciate art and to meet other kids with the same interests. Devoting the extra room in the gallery for their use was a dream come true for him.

So far, the teen center was bare bones: just some old couches, a collection of excellent large-format books about art, a CD player, a soda machine, and some art supplies kids could use when they were in the building. Even without a lot to offer, the teen center was becoming a really cool place to be after school and on weekends.

And whenever Phil hung a new exhibition of kids' artwork, the community supported it with a big turnout. So far, not a lot of people were *buying* from the gallery, but he appreciated the interest.

Cindi and Noah finally caught up with Shelby two blocks away from the gallery.

"Wait up," Cindi called to her. "What are you thinking?"

"I'm thinking maybe the break-in was a deliberate move to put the gallery's future in jeopardy—to put it out of business," Shelby answered her.

"Explain," Noah asked.

"Think about it," she continued. "I figure there are three prime suspects. Dr. Taylor was at the gallery the day Cindi's photo was hung, so he knew it was there. And he practically threatened Phil in public. He would be in a pretty good position to get his hands on the paintings he wanted if your uncle had to sell out quick to vacate the property.

"And what about Gerald Vincent?" Shelby went on. "He wants the gallery to fail so he can get twice the rent from a frozen yogurt business."

Cindi nodded. Shelby's reasoning made sense. They were running now, and the gallery loomed ahead of them.

"Anybody else?" Cindi asked.

"You're not going to believe it," Shelby answered. "But I suspect Janis Pine."

"Janis Pine? The crabby lady next door to the

gallery?'' asked Noah. ''You think she ripped the door off the wall and stole the photograph? How? Why?''

''How, I don't know,'' Shelby answered. ''But she was at C.J.'s the night the photo was stolen. She hates kids. And she hates the noise from the teen center. She could have set this whole thing up to get your uncle thrown out. Any one of the three suspects could have.''

''But how are you going to prove it?'' Cindi asked.

Shelby held up the stamp. ''With this.''

Remember what Phil said about writing the check to the insurance company...

''I distinctly remember putting it in the stack of mail on the front desk. It was the last check I wrote, the last one to go in an envelope and get sealed. I'm sure it went out with the other mail that day,'' he assured them.

The three kids rushed inside the gallery and found Cindi's uncle at the front desk.

''It's a long shot, I know,'' Shelby began. ''But

have you mailed anything since the day you put the insurance envelope in the pile?"

Phil thought a moment. "No, I don't think so. Why?"

Shelby was thinking about how her grandfather dealt with postage at the inn. "Do you buy your stamps in big rolls like my grandfather does?" she asked him.

Instead of answering, Phil pulled open the drawer of the desk and handed the roll to her. Shelby unfurled it enough to lay the first stamp on the roll alongside the stamp on the torn envelope from C.J.'s garbage. She had noticed the stamp on the envelope was torn a little. Whoever placed it there hadn't separated it perfectly at the perforations.

Her heart beat faster when she lined it up next to the stamp on the roll. Sure enough—it was a perfect match! The stamp had been torn from Phil's roll. She held it up to the others to see.

"Here, take a look," Shelby said.

Noah looked at the filthy stamp. "I can see all right from here," he told her.

"But it still doesn't make sense," Cindi's uncle told them. "I took the mail to the post office myself that day. I'm sure I mailed the insurance payment."

"Didn't you have a reminder on your bulletin board that the payment was due?" Shelby asked.

"The note was there a full week," Phil replied.

"Anyone could have seen the note," Noah said, realizing where Shelby was heading. "And since the address on the payment slip shows through the window on the envelope, anyone looking at the stuff on your desk would have known it was your bill payment."

"That guy Vincent seemed pretty interested in the stuff on your desk," Cindi said, remembering him looking at Phil's documents earlier.

"He's pretty nosy," Phil told her.

Noah explained the rest of Shelby's suspicions to Cindi's uncle. "Shelby thinks this was a deliberate plot to get you in trouble with the insurance company, so you'd lose the gallery."

"Well, if that was the plan, it could work," Phil said. "I didn't want you kids to worry before. But I've been thinking it over. Even auctioning off the Dorot might not save the business."

"Oh, Uncle Phil!" Cindi cried. "It's the painting you love so much."

Shelby looked at the clock. "I'm so unbelievably late for work," she told them. "I'm telling Detective Hineline about everything as soon as I get there."

Breaking into someone's store and stealing something was bad enough. Tampering with the mail made the crime a federal offense.

"Tell me, Shelby, how many people handled this stamp?" the detective questioned her. "Was it just Will, and you, and Cindi's uncle, *and* the thief, or did you pass it around in school for 'Show-and-Tell'?"

Shelby tried not to let the detective see she disliked the sarcasm. "Detective, I'm in high school, and we don't have 'Show-and-Tell,' " she responded evenly. "But I get your point. I'm sorry. I shouldn't have touched it. It came from the garbage and was covered with muck. I didn't know you could still gather any evidence off it."

"Well, we'll never know now," he told her.

Shelby could see he didn't have much interest in following up on what she had discovered. He listened to her theories about the case, but was called away to investigate an assault before she could ask what he made of it.

Her work didn't hold much interest for her that day. There was a lot of filing. Some pamphlets from the federal government had to be inserted into each law officer's mail cubbyhole. She just trudged through it until it was time to go home.

When she arrived at the inn, the phone was ringing. She called for her grandfather, then remembered he had gone to a movie and would be home after her.

Dropping her school books on the kitchen table, she reached for the receiver with one hand and with the other, pulled open the refrigerator.

"Easterly Breeze," Shelby said. She waited, but the line was quiet. "Hello?" She said again, "Easterly Breeze."

"I'm looking for Shelby Woo," said the voice on the other end of the line.

"Speaking," said Shelby, grabbing a bottle of juice from the refrigerator.

"I was expecting a man," the voice said.

"It's a girl's name, too," she said. "Who is this?"

The voice was muffled and, she realized later, disguised. It was probably the voice of a man, but it could have been an older woman's, too.

"I have a riddle for you: What happens to inquisitive little girls who don't mind their business? The answer is, you don't want to find out."

The voice was silent a moment. Then it continued. "Stay out of that break-in at the gallery. This is your only warning."

And then the phone went dead.

Chapter
6

At school the next day, kids kept coming up to Cindi to ask what they could do to save the teen center. Word had spread that Phil expected to auction off his only valuable painting, and still might not hold on to his business. The kids talked about a benefit dance, a car wash, a huge yard sale . . .

"This is great," Cindi told Shelby after last period. "There's a ton of interest. I don't think Uncle Phil has anything to worry about."

Shelby nodded and smiled slightly, and Cindi could tell something was wrong.

"What's up?" she asked. Shelby gulped hard. She had decided not to tell her grandfather or the detective about the strange phone call. They would probably want her off the case if they knew she was in any danger. But she told her friend all about the muffled voice and the threat.

"There's only one explanation," Shelby said. "One of my suspects must know I'm on the case."

Detective Hineline was out when she showed up for work, but he had left her some assignments.

Every job includes tasks that never seem to get mentioned before an employee is hired. For Cindi, who loved leafing through other people's pictures as they popped off the printing machine, the most hated part of work at the photo shop was alphabetizing the little bags of prints. And Noah couldn't stand—well, basically anything involving customers.

But for the young, part-time clerk at the Cocoa Beach Police Department, what she disliked most was inventory. Knowing how many "number two" pencils, reams of preprinted missing property forms, or cases of paper towels were on hand was probably important to someone, but Shelby just couldn't see the vital connection between inventory and law enforcement.

She welcomed visitors and distraction. That was why she was delighted to see Detective Hineline pass the squad room and head in her direction.

"Oh, Shelby, here you are," he began strangely, as if he was surprised to find her with her legs tucked under her on the cold linoleum. He held a stack of business cards. "I was thinking about going to someone new for a haircut, and I was just wondering if you knew much about either of these two barbers."

"Uh—sure, Detective," she answered. This was unusual. Detective Hineline virtually never revealed anything about his private life to Shelby. But she was eager for the opportunity to meddle in anything relating to him, so she stood up and took the cards.

"Um, Boris Ankor, I would definitely stay away from," she told him, inspecting the first one. "Have you ever noticed all the World War II memorabilia in his window? All those unexploded grenades and rusty bayonets? What if he has a flashback or something? That's a guy I wouldn't want near my ears with shears."

She looked at the second card. "Tony Litre. Some kids at school go to him. Depends if you like the look that's his specialty—you know, fuzz-on-top, shaved-skull-below. Works for some guys, if you've got the ears for it." She looked at the detective. "You might want to consider some other options," she suggested.

She didn't mean it as an insult. She wondered if the detective took it as one.

"Well, okay, thanks," he told her, appearing genuinely grateful for the advice.

As Shelby stepped onto a stool to reach a box of envelopes on a high shelf, she saw the detective riffle through the other cards he held. "You know, it's really a great convenience that everyone in town puts business cards on the wall at C.J.'s," he said. "For instance, if you need a new roof, there's Jimmy Sunshine's card. If you need a taxi, here's a card from A-1 Cabs."

He flipped to the next card. "And if you have any information about the break-in and theft of a photograph from the Horizon Art Center, here's the number to call to reach Shelby Woo."

The envelopes crashed to the floor as Shelby grabbed the side of the doorjamb to steady herself.

"*What?*" she asked, incredulous.

Detective Hineline held up a card from the

Crazee Beat Surf Shop and turned it over to show her the handwritten message on the back.

"You got this at C.J.'s?" she asked, her heart thumping.

"You know I did," he answered. "It was right where you put it, for everyone to see."

She started to protest, but recalled something from her visit to C.J.'s the day the burglary was discovered.

Cindi took a business card off the wall near the phone where it was tacked, turned it over, and set it down on the counter. She started to write something on the back. But Shelby was in too much of a hurry to ask what it was.

"Of course," said Shelby, not even realizing she was speaking. "And that's the answer to the other question, too—the voice on the phone."

"What voice?" the detective asked, concerned.

Shelby realized she had blurted out too much. If she told the detective about the warning she'd got, he would certainly demand to know what the caller said. And then he'd certainly tell her to stop investigating.

"Oh—just some silly call. Kind of a joke, I

guess. I wondered how the person knew my first name, since the phone is under my grandfather's name. You know, why don't I just take that card and—''

She reached for it, but the detective ripped it in two. Instead of scolding her for the umpteenth time, he took a deep breath. His tone was quiet and sympathetic when he finally spoke.

''Shelby, this is difficult, but it's a fact. A lot of crimes just don't get solved, despite our efforts. We search for clues, talk to anyone we suspect, canvass the neighborhood for witnesses, look at crime records to find similar crimes—and sometimes we get lucky. Sometimes, someone calls us and gives us a tip.''

Shelby nodded. She knew firsthand from hanging around the station how often the difference between solving a crime and not solving it came down to a report from a concerned citizen.

Shelby reminded the detective about all the clues she had uncovered: Dr. Taylor's interest in the painting, and his threat; Vincent, the landlord, wanting Phil out of the building, and how they saw him touching stuff on Phil's desk; Janis Pine's hatred of kids, and the fact that she was seen at C.J.'s the night of the burglary; and, most important of all, how the missing photograph showed up in C.J.'s' trash, right next to the envelope that had to have been stolen off Phil's front desk.

The detective listened, then went on with his speech. "If Dr. Taylor wanted the painting, why didn't he steal it?" the detective asked. "Besides, a neighbor saw his car drive into his driveway that night, and his gate never opened again until morning." He saw the surprise in Shelby's eyes. "Yes, despite what you think, we *do* go out and investigate."

"Then what about the landlord, Gerald Vincent? Or the neighbor, Ms. Pine? They could have set the whole thing up," she insisted.

"Yes, except Gerald Vincent was seen at Looney's Lounge earlier in the evening the night of the break-in, and something he ate made him sick. He couldn't even drive home. I spoke to the taxi driver myself. And Ms. Pine has a lot of trouble seeing at night because of her eyes," the detective explained. "I know because we talked to a woman who prepares her letters and helps her with her banking. Seems unlikely she would be out at night poking around alone in a dark gallery, don't you think?"

Yes, Shelby thought. *They all sound like good alibis*. Not without holes, though. The doctor could have sneaked out without his car. Janis Pine could have come in when it was light and memorized the layout of the gallery—Shelby had employed that technique herself in her investigating. And Vincent could have been faking. She had seen Noah acting sick in a play one year, and it was totally convincing.

Shelby listened while the detective finished.

"Shelby, we've got other cases. And when the boss says 'move on,' we move on." Detective Hineline was referring to his commanding officer at the station. "To tell you the truth, looking at this thing realistically, I have to say it seems more like a prank than anything else. If I were you, I'd be more interested in *Cindi's* enemies than in her uncle's."

Of course, the idea that anyone would hate Cindi for anything was ridiculous, and the detective knew that.

"But all you should be interested in right now is cleaning up this messy closet. If this case gets solved, Shelby, it'll be solved by the police. No more business cards. Okay?"

Shelby nodded unenthusiastically. The detective bent, scooped up the envelopes, and handed them to her.

Back at her desk, Shelby called Cindi. She was the only one who could have posted the card at C.J.'s.

"What did you think when I got that threatening call?" Shelby asked her. "You didn't see the connection to the card you posted?"

"I never thought the bad guy would call," Cindi said, "just people trying to help. And I guess I just forgot about all the cards."

" 'All the cards'?" Shelby asked her. "You mean, there were others? Besides at C.J.'s?"

"I posted a few more. Like, at the grocery stores and the laundromat. And near the water tube rental shack. Oh, and at the pier. Yeah, definitely at the pier. And at the first aid station, too. And—"

Shelby cut off her friend. "Cindi, the detective is going to kill me! He thinks *I* put those cards up."

"You know, I've got a break coming up,"

Cindi said quickly, "and if I hurry, I can probably get all of them down before—"

"Not probably, Cindi. Not probably! Absolutely!" Shelby said. "Every last one of them!"

"I'm on my way!" Cindi vowed. "Sorr-ee!"

Detective Hineline bought Shelby dinner that night. It was unusual for her to stay at the police station so late, but the police radio wouldn't stop squawking one emergency after another, and someone had to hang around to wait for the truck delivering the department's new air conditioners.

She called her grandfather to tell him she would do her homework at her desk and be home later, and Mike Woo gave his approval. For Shelby, it was an opportunity to see the department at an hour when she was usually at home, peacefully reading or watching a movie on TV.

Nighttime at the police department was anything but peaceful. Even in the rare moments when the phone wasn't ringing and cars weren't being dispatched, a quiet urgency hung over the office that evening. Casual conversations were quick, as if people knew better than to get involved in long stories. The next call could be about a crisis that would keep an officer busy the rest of the night.

Maybe because of the potential for danger lurking in nighttime crimes, the police officers enjoyed a camaraderie Shelby never noticed in the after-school hours she normally worked. The office was a hearth that drew its special family close and warm, sheltered from the cold reality outside the department's walls. The officers even joked with Shelby, making her feel a part of it all. With most of her real family so far away, except for her grandfather, Shelby loved belonging to the family of law enforcers. She could stay with the department forever.

But finally, it was time for her to go. She made a fresh pot of coffee for the overnight crew, then walked around the office scattering sharp pencils and other supplies on desks to take advantage of the opportunity to chat a bit with each of the detectives and officers, catching up on their cases and wishing them good night. They all found it easy to talk to Shelby, undoubtedly because she wanted so much to learn from their experience and methods.

Shelby punched into the phone the number of

the Easterly Breeze. When her grandfather answered, she told him she had decided to walk home. It wasn't that late yet, and the route to her house was safe. Mike said it was fine with him.

Outside, Shelby could hear the voices and laughter of people partying at one of Cocoa Beach's many late spots. She turned away from the noise toward home, walked a short way, then doubled back in the opposite direction. She wanted to see the Horizon Art Center at night. Maybe there was something special about the gallery in darkness that could reveal a new clue about the crime. She wasn't investigating, she told herself, practicing the lie she would tell Detective Hineline if he found out. It was a nice night for a stroll, and she was just taking the long way home.

To her surprise, Shelby found she was not the only one checking out the place. She was still a good hundred feet away from the building when she noticed a figure peering into a window of the gallery.

Her eyes widened when she recognized who it was: the woman in the broad-brimmed straw hat, whom Shelby had nearly knocked over that day, leaving C.J.'s! What was she doing at the scene of the crime? Staying out of sight, Shelby watched her walk next door to the tourist shop and pull on its locked door. Was she trying now to break into that place, too? Then the woman walked around the corner into the narrow alley dividing the two businesses. Unable to stop herself, Shelby followed.

Doing her best to become a part of the wall, Shelby moved toward her. She took a deep breath, then peeked around the corner. The woman had disappeared!

Puzzled, Shelby took a few tentative steps. Seeing nothing, she walked quickly, hoping she didn't lose the woman out the other end. Shelby was nearly at the end of the alley, where it opened into a rear parking lot, when a noise behind her caught her off guard.

It was a side door of the gift shop opening. The woman with the straw hat *had* broken in! And she was coming back out!

Shelby needed to hide. But there were no other doors. All she saw was an open Dumpster. Oh well—she was in no position to be picky.

She closed the distance between herself and the Dumpster in a few long strides, grabbed the rim of the bin, and hoisted herself over the top.

She couldn't believe the smell; it almost made her faint. And she didn't want to look too closely at whatever it was that cushioned her landing.

But what Shelby didn't realize until it was too late was that the alleyway was constructed on a bit of an incline, and the Dumpster was on wheels. Despite her small size, Shelby's leap was just forceful enough to set the Dumpster moving!

With a lurch to her stomach, she felt the Dumpster begin to roll. The garbage receptacle was on its way to the parking lot, with Shelby bouncing around inside amid the muck and the trash!

Chapter 7

 The card.

Why, the thief asked again and again, *why am I letting it bother me?*

The photograph meant nothing. It wasn't just worthless. It was worthless and *in the way*. Using a knife to slice it from the frame had been child's play. Discarding it behind that ratty burger joint was another decision made thoughtlessly and effortlessly. Most likely it would never be found—the thief had been certain. If found, it almost certainly wouldn't be retrieved. If retrieved, the chances were slim at best that it would be displayed. And be recognized? Who could recognize such a photograph?

Even if it were recognized, there was absolutely, positively, no chance at all a connection could be made, *ever*, to the thief.

But someone was trying.

The card.

The first one appeared tacked above the pay phone at the burger joint itself where, wonder of wonders, the photograph had reappeared. That had been startling enough, seeing that photograph again.

Did my face register the shock? the thief wondered. *Did anyone notice? Was my mind quick enough to cover the reaction?*

Before the day was out, the card, with its little note asking for help in finding the thief, was joined by others. They were multiplying almost by the hour.

The cards seem to be following me around town, the thief thought. *There's nowhere to look without seeing them. Like the eyes of my pursuer, watching me . . . Waiting for me to make a mistake.*

That could never happen. The crime was too well-planned. What hour to strike. How to gain entry. The path to take behind the gallery, and which alley would lead most directly and least suspiciously to the rear of the burger joint.

Deciding which piece to steal from the show was not part of the plan. The thief couldn't have known it was the work of the gallery owner's niece. But it didn't matter at all to the thief which photograph or painting from that amateur show was stolen. Didn't matter at all.

What mattered was that the job was done, no clues were left behind, the cops weren't getting too nosy, and no one could associate the crime with the thief who had committed it.

The card.

I've got to stop gnawing at myself about that card, the thief thought. But it was nearly impossible. It was like someone saying, "Think about anything except an elephant." To have carried out a crime so perfectly and entirely undetected, and then to be so obsessed with a silly card. It was unnerving.

Shelby Woo. What possible threat could she be? Why, she's just a girl, the thief reasoned.

But what course to follow next?

I mustn't act too hastily, thought the thief. *So far, so good.* Better to watch and wait, try to learn what her capabilities might be. The lucky amateur couldn't be entirely discounted.

After all, I'm no professional art thief, and so far, everything is working out perfectly.

Except for that card.

The card asked for phone calls. Whoever posted the card had been thoughtful enough to include her phone number, so that looking it up in the directory would be unnecessary. Well, the thief had made a call. Not the kind of call the young girl was expecting, but certainly the call she deserved for meddling in someone else's business.

That was a good place to start. Just a simple call, warning her. She thought this was about a photograph? No, this was not a crime about a photograph. This was bigger business than she could ever imagine. Business that could get her hurt.

Of course, harming the girl was a step the thief would hate to take. *I have nothing against her. Why is she so determined to hurt me?*

Her nosiness could provide the obvious solution. All sorts of "accidents" could be arranged, completely unrelated to the thief. A hit-and-run on a deserted street, for example. *Do you use your own car, or rent one for that purpose?* the thief wondered. *Would hiring an accomplice be a mistake?*

Or should she just disappear? That had been known to happen.

It was silly to be so obsessed. The warning call

would probably be enough. But if the warning call didn't have the intended effect . . .

There would have to be a plan, of course. It wouldn't do at all to strike at her without a careful plan. Carelessness could lead to discovery. The newspapers were filled each day with stories about otherwise perfect crimes, undone by carelessness. The thief would begin planning immediately.

That had been the reason everything so far had been so well carried-out. The thief's lips curled into a smile. A well-executed plan was like a gorgeous glass figurine. Simple, delicate, transparent, but full of color and intricate detail.

Suddenly, a thought blew through the thief's mind like a chill wind and shattered the smile as easily as glass.

Have I been careless? Is there some detail I missed? Will she find it before I remember?

The thief tried to relax and remember all the good that would come from the plan set in motion. But Shelby Woo was an elephant, consuming the thief's thoughts.

Why am I so concerned with the meddling actions of a simple schoolgirl?

Chapter
8

Shelby's grandpa, with all his knowledge of natural science, would say the assault on Shelby's nose inside the Dumpster was just the result of the normal process of decomposition. As a criminalist in San Francisco, he had probably experienced much worse.

Hanging on for dear life, she tried to hold her breath so she wouldn't smell the stench, but soon needed to gasp for air. She'd never smelled anything as bad as the inside of the Dumpster.

Not only was the smell enough to spin her eyes in her head, but the noise of the wheels, clattering across the parking lot, deafened Shelby. The wheels squealed and scraped against the asphalt, the metal lid crashed and smashed.

Uh-oh. What was it Shelby suddenly heard over the clanging metal lid, louder than the squeal of the wheels catching on the Dumpster's warped bottom?

It sounded like an engine. A very big engine, pulling a very large, lumbering vehicle. And in a flash, Shelby realized the real danger she faced.

The access road behind the gallery and gift shop, while usually deserted, was used for deliveries and garbage pickup—garbage that was usually picked up at night, after dark. Like, right about now.

Then she remembered the lights behind the gallery and gift shop were broken. Meaning it was extremely dark, darker than usual.

Shelby was in a runaway Dumpster, in almost total darkness, about to be hit by a hurtling garbage truck!

If only, Shelby thought. *If only it could happen just exactly that way. I'd be flattened completely, so I'd never have to see people chuckling over the headline in the Cocoa Beach Sentinel:* "Girl, Gaga for Garbage, Dies in Dumpster Drive."

This night, however, was not the night Shelby would be spared humiliation.

She had guessed right—it was a garbage truck, heading right for the spot her Dumpster would cross into traffic. But the parking lot's designer had been careful to include barriers to keep cars from rolling out into the road. Large logs, about the thickness of telephone poles lying on their sides, rimmed the perimeter of the area.

And that's what the Dumpster hit.

She wasn't moving fast, but the collision sent Shelby knocking against the side of the container. Because of the slope of the parking lot asphalt and the Dumpster's forward motion, the thing went toppling.

It landed on its side with a steely sound that echoed through the night silence. The Dumpster's metal mouth gaped, and in a great big heave, it belched out sacks of smelly trash and food waste. Tucked inside the pile, Shelby poured out onto the edge of the roadway.

The garbage truck's headlights hurled straight ahead, missing entirely the upheaval just inches from the rig's right tire. But the sound the crashing Dumpster made caused an almost instantaneous reflex in the driver. He swerved to the left, simultaneously sounding the deafening airhorn to vent anger and a warning at whatever it was that dared to challenge his course.

Safely out of the way, the driver slammed on the brakes. They squealed in the effort of stopping such an enormous vehicle. The driver opened his door and stepped out, peering over the cab of the truck.

Shelby was still more a part of the heap than she was a distinct individual. In the dim light, the driver never saw her. In all the years he had been transporting trash, this was the first time a Dumpster had raced out to greet him. Then he saw the old woman in the hat, who was walking toward the mess.

"I ain't cleaning that up," he called to her. "I haul it. I don't shovel it off the ground. Uh-uh. No ma'am."

He waited for her to argue, but she only looked even more bewildered than he did. Finally, he climbed into the cab, released the brake, and lumbered away.

Looking like some sort of prehistoric bird arising from a primordial swamp, Shelby slowly sat up in the garbage. Ugh! She lifted one arm, dripping with gunk, and dropped it again at her side. The stench rose up like a small cloud hovering right over her head.

Seeing Shelby sit up startled the woman with the broad-brimmed hat. Her eyes opened wide. Then her features strangled into a tight knot.

"I thought I told you garbage-picking, stinking tramps not to—" she began, walking briskly in Shelby's direction.

Shelby looked up. She would never have imagined anyone so tiny and frail could move so fast, but the woman seemed propelled across the lot by her fury. Then she was standing over Shelby, squinting in the darkness. And her hard gaze seemed to relax.

"Why, you're just a kid!"

Shelby looked up at her, still a little dazed, still covered with garbage from head to foot. Is it possible? Shelby wondered. Is it possible she doesn't recognize me from the other day near C.J.'s? The sun was so bright that day, and now it's so dark. Not to mention the rubbish obscuring much of her face. In all Shelby's crime-solving adventures, she had never before considered garbage as the perfect disguise.

"You poor dear. You must be starving to be rummaging around in this thing," the woman continued. "But where are your people? Are you from around here? If you're hungry, child, take this."

She had mistaken Shelby for a poor child, desperate for money and a meal.

The woman reached into her purse, picked through her personal items, and brought out a five-dollar bill. She held it out to Shelby.

The kind gesture from a woman Shelby thought was so cruel and angry surprised her. Not to mention the strange surprise of having someone think she needed charity. At first, she didn't know what to say.

She tried to refuse. "Thanks, but I don't—"

"Sure you do," the older woman insisted. "That's all right. It's not much, but you can get yourself a nice bowl of soup at C.J.'s. They have good soup."

Yeah, right, Shelby thought. That's just what I want down my throat. A steaming bowl of the same stuff I'm sitting in. Eating the soup at C.J.'s is like—

Soup. Wait a minute. Soup? Soup!

Where had I heard about someone liking C.J.'s soup? It was just a few days ago, right after Cindi's photograph was stolen.

"Every day for lunch, Janis Pine comes in for soup," Will answered. "After she closes the gift shop at night, she gets another cup to take home."

That's it!

Will had told Shelby, Cindi, and Noah about the people at the burger joint the night the picture disappeared. This could only be one woman—Janis Pine, owner of the gift shop next to the gallery!

When Shelby had heard the side door of the gift shop open just a few minutes ago, what she heard was the woman coming out of her own shop.

Suddenly, the woman was talking to Shelby again. "You look like a nice girl. Not like those rowdy kids who loiter at the gallery next door, scaring away my trade. I'd do anything to have that place closed for good. But never mind, never mind—just take this."

Shelby pulled her filthy body away.

"Oh, now, I'm not worried about a little garbage," Janis said, grabbing Shelby's hands and pressing the bill into them with her own. Shelby looked at the woman's hands. She was struck by their softness and strength. Beautiful hands, strangely unlined for a woman Janis's age, Shelby noted. Hands that communicated something vital and caring.

Not wanting to prolong the conversation any longer for fear Janis would recognize her, Shelby accepted the gift. The inn had a canister for charity on the registration desk. She'd make a five-dollar donation.

"Thank you, ma'am," Shelby said, looking away to the ground. "You're very kind."

The woman's face, which had eased while she talked to Shelby, crinkled into a scowl again.

"No, I'm not, and don't you dare tell those other lousy kids I am," she barked out at the girl.

Her tone startled Shelby. Was she joking? Or did she really hate kids? And if she did, why was she being so nice to Shelby?

Shelby didn't want to stick around to find out. As quickly as she could, she scrambled up and away.

"Wait!" Janis called after her. "You can't walk into a restaurant like that. You've got to clean up. Where do you live? Who minds you, girl? Come back!"

Slipping and sliding, Shelby ran. At first she was disoriented. As strange as it seemed, four years of living in Cocoa Beach couldn't help her find the ocean, that's how furiously her mind was racing. She tried sniffing to detect the salt in the air, but all she could smell was the odor of her own clothes.

She had to get to the ocean. As difficult as it would be to wade in, clothes on, and race home through the cold night air, she had no choice. She wanted to get the garbage germs off Amber's scratch on her wrist, which was starting to itch. And there's no way she could walk into the bed-and-breakfast smelling like a sewer. They had guests. Not to mention Grandpa.

When Shelby's grandpa heard the door open, he lowered his newspaper into his lap and looked up at the entrance. His granddaughter stood there, dripping wet, shivering from the evening air. He sat, stunned.

"Shelby, what on earth—!" he sputtered, rising.

She tried to smile, but her chattering teeth and blue lips could barely hold the pose. "You know, you g-g-g-gotta be c-c-c-careful whose lawns you c-c-c-cross when it's dark outside," she lied. "Those auto-m-m-matic sprinklers can be m-m-m-murder!"

Mike put his arms around the trembling girl and pulled her toward the kitchen, where he could fetch some warm, dry towels.

He suddenly remembered the Koenigsbergs, a husband and wife, who had been sitting at the chess set, engrossed in a game. Mr. Koenigsberg's hand held a castle high above the board. His eyes were locked on Shelby and Mike.

Mike smiled awkwardly. "Sprinklers," he repeated, knowing his guests didn't believe the explanation either. "Could happen to anybody."

He smiled again, but Mr. Koenigsberg's hand remained frozen, as did his gaze. Averting his eyes, Mike hustled his granddaughter away from the guests.

"I didn't embarrass you, did I, Grandpa?" Shelby started as she toweled off her hair. "I'm so sorry the Koenigsbergs saw me like this."

"That's what you are sorry about?" Mike replied.

"What do you mean, Grandpa?"

"What I mean is, the Koenigsbergs were telling me earlier they have a daughter just about your age, so my guess is very little shocks them," he continued. "Your problem is not with the Koenigsbergs."

"You're mad, aren't you?" she asked.

"Depends," he answered.

"On what?"

"How long you're going to stick with that silly excuse that you ran through somebody's sprinkler." He looked at her with eyes like piercing laser lights.

Why do I even try lying to him, she wondered. *I don't know how he always knows, but he always knows.*

"Grandpa, how important is one person to a town? Or one business?" she asked, avoiding his gaze.

Mike blinked. *Where was this going?* he wondered. "There is one measure I know," he answered. "How much they are missed when they are gone."

8 2

A Slash in the Night

Shelby looked seriously at her grandfather. "There's a place in town I think is pretty important," she told him. "But if we have to lose it to find out, I guess I'd rather not know the answer to my question."

Mike's eyes narrowed. He could press her for information. But details were unimportant. He knew of her recent adventure, and her concerns could only be about the gallery Cindi's uncle might lose. And the teen center the kids in the community would have to do without.

This is partially my fault, Mike Woo thought. *All those letters I sent, exciting her about my cases.* He worried about her. But he knew she was hooked on solving her own mysteries.

Inside his head, two voices warred. *I really should trust her to know what is and isn't safe*, said the first. *After all, she's not a child anymore, like she was when she first came here.*

Another part of his brain sounded a more ominous tone. *She is just a child—your granddaughter*, it told him. *If anything ever happened to her, you would never forgive yourself.*

It was difficult—impossible—to be everything a child needed from an adult. *What does Shelby need tonight?* Mike wondered. Discipline? Understanding? Or just warm clothes?

Mike hugged her. He sniffed.

"Maybe tomorrow, after school, you should think about shopping for some new shampoo," he told her. "What is it you are using on your hair?"

Not knowing what he suspected, but knowing he cared, Shelby squeezed her grandfather. She slipped up the back stairs, glancing down at Mike just long enough for her eyes to say, "Don't worry." His eyes answered, "I will always worry. It's my job to worry."

"You know, Shelby, I'm really surprised at you," Noah chided her. "Don't you remember all those lectures we sat through in health class? 'Don't lend someone your comb . . . cover your mouth when you cough . . . never joyride inside a Dumpster.' "

"I must have been absent on Dumpster day," she answered him.

Shelby smoothed her clothes as they walked down the hall from chemistry class. She had chosen her short camouflage skirt with one of her grandfather's pressed white dress shirts as her outfit for school that morning. Something about the previous night's ride made her want to be very neat and tailored that day.

They joined Cindi at her locker. "Was Bucky's quiz hard?" she asked them, flipping pages of her textbook. "Bucky" was the name they all called Mr. Bucchiero, the chemistry teacher.

"Sherman Whitlock was finished in, like, twelve minutes," Noah said. Sherman was the smartest kid in their class. Everyone else would still be chewing their nails, and Sherman's test would be on the teacher's desk, his nose buried in a comic book. But most quizzes took him only eight minutes, Cindi knew. She started flipping pages even more furiously.

Knowing Cindi needed the time to cram, Shelby quickly reported on her activities the previous evening.

"Janis Pine sounds like a pretty good suspect in the gallery break-in," Cindi said after she heard the account. "Look at the sign on her door, warning kids to stay out of her store. And what was it she told you?"

She did say something interesting...

"You look like a nice girl. Not like those noisy, rowdy kids who loiter at the gallery next door, scaring away my trade. I'd do anything to have that place closed for good."

"When she said she'd do anything, that could include breaking in and stealing my picture so the gallery could get in financial trouble," Cindi said.

Noah had a different opinion. "Does that really sound like something a woman her age could do?" he asked. "Breaking a door like that takes some muscle."

"You're assuming because she's old, she's frail," Shelby replied. "She held my hands, and hers were not the hands of someone who needed help with anything."

Cindi pressed on, chemistry forgotten. "Sounds like she had a pretty good motive, and the ability to carry it out. What about opportunity?"

"Well, we know she was at C.J.'s the night the photograph disappeared," Shelby said.

"Yeah, but what does that prove? She's there every night," Noah reminded him.

Shelby admitted the truth in that. She told her

friends there wasn't any other choice but to investigate the other suspects.

"Well, we better do something fast," Cindi said. "I called home at lunchtime, and my mom says Uncle Phil set the date to auction off his painting. It's in three days."

"That soon?" Shelby asked.

"And he's not even sure he'll get enough money for it to save the gallery before his lease is up," Cindi added. "Vincent's kicking him out next week."

"Three days," Shelby repeated. "That doesn't give us much time."

Noah reminded Shelby that Detective Hineline had said to stay out of the investigation. But Shelby corrected him. "What he actually said was, not to put up any more cards. And I haven't, right? So listen, I've got an idea."

Chapter
9

Far down the list of attractions in Central Florida—after the theme parks, the cultural institutions, and NASA's museums and exhibits; below the nature walks, wildlife preserves, parks, and historic trails; way down beneath the restored plantations and the citrus groves; even a good bit lower down than such rip-offs as The Zany Funhouse, The Soap Museum, and Michele's Seashells—came Space Coast Speedway.

You had to look hard to find it. The broken down go-carts at Space Coast Speedway buzzed a noisy lure far off the beaten track of the more popular tourist destinations, such as the famous pier and the even more famous surf shops.

In fact, one unlucky group of potential visitors was its chief target: vacationers who called their travel agents too late to reserve rooms in one of the many fine motels and hotels along the beach. They were stuck staying at Cosmic Cabins, an awful collection of leaky, drafty, termite traps directly across the street from the go-cart track.

Space Coast Speedway could always count on enough poor souls from the cabins, desperately looking for some activity close to where they were staying, to remain in business.

"I came to a birthday party here one year when I was little," Noah remembered as Cindi parked her car and they looked up at the ticket building. "Parents were dropping kids off, and kids were crying. They knew there was going to be cake, and they were crying anyway."

"Well, bury those happy childhood memories. We have to make Gerald Vincent believe his business will soon be booming big-time or the plan won't fly," Shelby reminded him.

A sign on the door of the ticket office spelled out the terms. "$7.50 per half hour. One minute over, you pay the extra half. No exceptions!" Shelby knocked on the door, and Gerald Vincent's voice answered from inside the building.

"Closed for repairs," he said.

"And a very good afternoon to you, too," Noah muttered under his breath.

Cindi put her hand over his mouth as she whispered a warning for him to be quiet. "Just play your part. Let us do the rest of the talking," she said.

Shelby tried to peer in through the broken screen door. "Actually, Mr. Vincent, we're not here to race," she called.

"Then scram!" he shot back

"But we'd like to talk with you about an important matter," Cindi said.

"Oh, I'm sorry," the track owner replied, his voice dripping with sarcasm. "I didn't realize it was important." He made no move toward the door.

"Okay. Sorry to bother you," Shelby said cheerily. The kids started walking down the stairs. Shelby continued speaking, louder than usual, to make sure Vincent heard her inside his office.

"Come on, guys. Let's drive over to Rocket Park," she said, naming a more desirable go-cart track closer to the action.

"That's a waste of time," Cindi said, glancing

over her shoulder at the door. "I don't think that place can handle 300 kids in one afternoon."

"It's our last chance," Shelby answered. "We have to try to persuade them."

As the friends kept walking, Vincent's head appeared in the doorway. Through his round, black-framed glasses, he watched them continue on toward Cindi's car.

"I keep telling you we should cut the list. Make it 250, or even 200," Cindi said. "Three hundred kids is just too much. No place will want an event that large."

Vincent looked around at his empty go-cart track, then he spoke. "Hey, you kids, come here."

Cindi turned, as Shelby and Noah kept walking. "Who, us?" she asked.

"No, my Aunt Fanny," he said. "What's this about 300 kids?"

Shelby caught Noah's arm and pulled him around. "It'll only be for one afternoon, we promise," she called. "Just for one party."

"I said, come here," he called out to them again. Cindi was beginning to wonder if they were tangling with the wrong guy.

Shelby, still holding onto Noah, started speaking before she reached the stairs. "This is our friend, Lennie," she said, pointing to Noah, "and he'd shake your hand, except in this heat he tries not to exert himself."

"Who said anything about wanting to shake his hand?" Vincent said. "What's this about, anyway?"

Shelby turned to Noah. "Is the sun too much for you, Lennie? Should we get you someplace shady?"

Vincent looked at them on the other side of the door. The man didn't know that Noah was working hard, trying to remember all the techniques he used in last year's class play, where he never spoke a line, but was on stage from the minute the curtain opened until it closed. The character he played had been in a car accident, and all the action took place around him. But that was last year. And it was a play. Could he make it look real enough in life?

"You can come in," Vincent told them, kicking the door open with his foot.

Shelby's trained eyes quickly scanned the room and recorded mental notes. The indoor/outdoor carpeting was stained, maybe from coffee, and smelled bad. Big, thick manuals, like telephone books, spilled off the shelves. Bills poured out of one of the file drawers under the desk, clearly in no order and clearly ignored. Take-out food containers and milk shake cups dribbled goo onto every visible counter space.

"What's his problem?" Vincent asked as Noah slumped against the wall.

"He gets tired real fast." Shelby thought to herself that her lie was actually half true.

"He's gotta lie down all the time," Cindi said.

Noah smiled slightly and waved to Vincent, who was staring at him. "So what's with the 300 kids?" Vincent asked, his mind shifting easily to the profit he would make from a group that large.

"Graduation party," said Cindi.

"We're on the committee," Shelby said.

"Graduation?" the track owner asked. "It's October."

"All the best places get booked up if you wait too long," Cindi replied. She turned to Noah. "Lennie, you rest here, okay, honey? We'll talk to the man outside."

Noah tried not to react. *Honey? What am I, four? If I'm good, do I get a lollipop?* he wondered silently.

"Who said he could rest here?" Vincent asked.

Cindi leaned in close to the track owner, pretending she didn't want Noah to hear. "Don't blow it. It's a surprise birthday party for Lennie." She leaned back out again. "So let's take a quick tour of the facilities," she said. "Don't worry about Lennie. He'll rest up and be as good as new. Well, as good as he gets, anyway."

"We don't want to take too much of your time," Shelby said.

She and Cindi each took one of Vincent's arms and pulled him out the door of the ticket office, while his eyes darted first over one shoulder, then over the other, back at Noah. The girls escorted the stocky man across the dry, dusty field to the track entrance.

Meanwhile, Noah sprang into action. The goal was to find the missing insurance check, just in case Vincent held onto it when he dumped the empty envelope. It could have been any place amid the clutter and debris.

"Oh well, I have to start somewhere," he muttered.

Outside, the girls were chattering about "Lennie."

"He gets depressed a lot, on account of being

tired all the time. That's why we're organizing the party," Shelby said.

"Right," said Cindi, "he's really a great guy once you get to know him."

"Who said I want to get to know him?" Vincent asked.

At the top of the track, go-carts of every color stood idle. More sat alongside the course, some without wheels, others just rusted shells planted in the dirt. Along one edge, the guardrail looked worn, and one wooden plank was missing. This place had definitely seen better days.

"So, what day would you want the place?" Vincent asked them.

"Um—well, that's not set yet," said Shelby. She looked back at the office, wondering if Noah had made any discoveries yet. Vincent seemed antsy, like he wanted them to leave. She had to keep the conversation going somehow. "We have to have our faculty advisor come and check the place out."

"Why's that?" asked Vincent. "I got a permit." He looked across the track at the place where the wooden rail was missing. "That, I could re-place in a minute if I needed to."

"Right," Cindi said. "Well, that's all right then."

Inside the office, Noah had finished flipping through the mail and, finding nothing out of the ordinary, decided to pull open the top drawer to the filing cabinet and continue his search there.

He didn't think his yank was all that strong, but the force of his tug pulled the front of the drawer clean off the rest of it, and sent Noah flying backward, landing him on the floor.

"Ohhh!" he groaned. "Ahh!" He stood up quickly and was back at the file cabinet, holding the drawer front against the rest of the drawer where it used to attach, trying to figure some way to get the severed metal to stay together.

Vincent heard the commotion, and Shelby had to stall for time. "Well, there's a good sign," she said. "He's feeling better already."

"Right," Cindi added. "He always makes that groaning sound when he starts improving."

Vincent paid them no attention. Curious about the sound coming from the office, he started walking back toward the screen door.

"You know, I think $7.50 per kid is a bargain," Shelby said, trying to steer him back. "The question I have is, are the cars fast enough? Because that's what kids really want."

Torn between his concerns over what was going on in the office, and his yearning for the money the girls seemed to be promising, Vincent halted in his tracks again.

"They're as fast as the laws allow," he told them.

"I'm sure they are," Shelby replied. "And that's perfectly acceptable to me. But the darn activities committee made me promise to try one out personally."

Vincent's eyes went back to the office, then again to Shelby. "It's okay with me if you do," he said. "Just stay away from the broken rail. And pay me the $7.50."

"Maybe you shouldn't. It doesn't look too safe, Shelby," Cindi said quietly.

Oops!

Simultaneously, the girls realized they should have talked about their scheme a little more thoroughly. They never had discussed using different names.

With all those cards Cindi had put up around town, and Shelby's phone threat, it occurred to them both that they could be in serious trouble if Gerald Vincent was the photo thief.

"Shelby," Vincent said, considering it. "What an unusual name. That's one I haven't heard very often."

"Only one in my class," Shelby said. She tried to take the focus away from it. "But there are three Jennifers. Which isn't to say it's not a nice name. I like the name Jennifer. Don't you?"

Vincent pointed to a car on the track. "Tell you what, Shelby," he said. "If it's speed you're after, try lucky number thirteen. Probably just what you're looking for."

Digging the $7.50 from her pocket, Shelby tried to think of a way out of taking the ride, but Vincent was already revving up the car.

Great, thought Noah inside the office. He was hoping for a little noise, so he could make some himself. He started rattling the drawer front against the drawer, trying to get it to at least rest against the cabinet and stay there.

The go-cart belched noxious smoke as it warmed up. "Come on, climb in," Vincent yelled over the noise.

"Don't I need a helmet or something?" Shelby hollered back at him.

"Naw, it's not required," he said. "And besides, they don't go *that* fast. Just hug the inside of the track, and you'll be fine."

"Now, you're sure this is your fastest car?" Cindi asked. She was beginning to wonder whether there was a particular reason Vincent had selected it. "I think that orange one over there looks a lot faster," she said.

"Is she going to take a ride or not?" the owner asked. Shelby had no choice. Gingerly, she climbed into the rig and sat down. She felt for the pedals. She looked out at the track, where it banked to the left and the right, noting where she'd have to slow for the turns.

Then, her right foot pressed the accelerator.

The car lurched ahead, throwing her body backward, with a little more force than she expected, and she gasped in surprise. The car packed some power, all right. But she had it quickly under control, at least through the first straightaway. Up ahead was a turn to the left, so Shelby's foot shifted to the brake.

Funny, she really expected the car to respond a little more promptly to her foot controls. Shelby bent her body all the way to the left, and crossed her right hand over her left on the steering wheel as she fought to keep the car restrained through the turn.

Halfway into the turn, she flung herself in the other direction to stay on top of the car. Weird! The thing didn't seem to slow down at all. *These cars must need a lot of braking room*, she thought. As a turn to the right approached, she decided to brake early and take the curve at leisure. Just past the turn was the section of guardrail that had to be replaced.

Her foot pressed the pedal. Again, the car did nothing in response.

Could I have mixed up the pedals? Shelby wondered. Even though she had her permit, Shelby never really practiced driving much, mostly because she didn't have a car yet. Or maybe things were backwards on a go-cart.

She pulled on the wheel and leaned to the right, getting into the turn well enough. But the turn was more extreme than the last one, the angle just a little sharper. She ran the left tires up onto the embankment.

"Shelby!" Cindi called. "Are you all right?"

Shelby couldn't hear her over the tiny engine's roar. She pulled the wheel again and jerked the car back onto the pavement. Nothing she did could slow it, however. Her hands were frozen in position, just trying to keep the car righted.

And just ahead was that section of missing guardrail.

"Turn!" she yelled at the cart. "Turn, turn, turn!"

But before she knew it, the car's front half climbed the grade and was leaving the track.

It headed straight down the bumpy hill toward route A1A, with Shelby clinging to it in terror.

Chapter
10

Every moment counted as Shelby's go-cart bounded down the hill, the danger increasing with each car-length. Yet, a part of her brain saw the entire situation as if it were happening in slow-motion, and she had all the time in the world to decide her course.

The highway? Her tiny go-cart wasn't a vehicle that would earn her a lot of respect on the open road. Cars coming from the south would be just through a long bend at the point they'd first see her, probably traveling dangerously fast. And even if the putting roadster had a warning horn, who would hear it?

She considered just trying to steer onto the

shoulder, but this was one stretch of the highway built without a shoulder. *Well, they probably saved a lot in tax dollars*, she thought, *although that's pretty small comfort now!*

The highway was out of the question. Which left her with: *the fence.* Positioned on either side of the track's property to separate it from its neighbors, the chain link fence was never intended as a lethal weapon, but Shelby imagined what it would feel like against the muscles and bones of her neck, if she continued moving as fast as she was.

For a moment her mind flashed on the key question: *WHAT AM I DOING HERE?* She cared a lot about Cindi, Cindi's uncle Phil, and the kids of Cocoa Beach, but did she care enough to be on a collision course with certain doom?

As doubtful as the result seemed, Shelby realized she had no chance against the oncoming cars, and only a slim one challenging the fence, but the fence it would have to be.

She pulled the steering wheel to the right and turned, gaining speed as she continued down the hill.

But then she saw something that made her wrest the wheel hard to the left again.

"Shelby!" screamed Cindi, "what are you doing?" She was running just ahead of Vincent.

Noah, inside the office, heard Cindi scream and knew something was wrong.

He was busy with some package sealing tape he had found, wadding it up so he could tape back the front of the file cabinet from the inside of the drawer, where the tape wouldn't be easily seen. From the looks of the office, it could be months before Vincent tried to pull out that drawer, and by then Noah, Cindi, and Shelby would be distant memories.

He would have liked to reinforce it, but the scream sounded urgent.

The screen door banged behind him as he raced out the door, his legs hitting the ground in one leap. At the far end of the track, he saw Cindi and Vincent disappearing as they raced down the hill out of his view. It wasn't very comforting to Noah to realize that Shelby was nowhere to be seen. Noah took off, desperately behind the others, running hard.

None of them saw what made Shelby suddenly decide to twist again away from the fence and toward the road: a patch of soft mud where the hill ended just before sloping up toward the highway again. Shelby hoped it was just soft enough, and just long enough, to stop the forward movement of the vehicle.

She didn't know for sure how fast she was going when the car hit the mud. But the cart rode so close to the ground that as soon as the wheels hit the soft earth, the cart bogged down and stopped dead.

Shelby felt herself continuing to fly forward, out of the cart and into the mud. *Oh, no. No way.* She was sick of doing laundry on this case. She held onto the wheel and braced her legs to keep herself wedged inside the vehicle.

The maneuver kept her in the seat, but the speed and the odd way she had to turn her leg forced it up against the side of the machine. She felt the metal scrape against her skin.

Looking down, she saw a little blood on her leg. She rocked her head from side to side. Her neck was still intact. She flexed her fingers and found that none were broken.

Just then, she looked up and saw a giant 18-wheeler rocket through the space her cart would have crossed. *And I would have hit like a bug on his windshield,* she thought.

A moment later, Cindi and Vincent, then Noah, were at her side.

"Shelby, are you all right?" Cindi asked.

Still shaking, Shelby answered, "Yeah. I scraped my leg a little, I guess. But it doesn't hurt."

Vincent lifted her out of the car and walked with her back up the hill. He hadn't said a word. The greedy man was too busy worrying about the possibility of a lawsuit for sticking a kid on an unsafe track.

Noah ran ahead of him to open the office door. He held it as Vincent walked through, holding Shelby. "You're looking a lot better," he said to Noah, wondering about his sudden recovery.

Noah caught his breath. "You know, sometimes a good emotional shock is all it takes," he said.

Vincent sat Shelby down on the couch and went to the sink in the small bathroom to wash his hands.

"I've got some stuff to patch that up," he told Shelby. "And a bandage. Used to cut myself, too, every once in a while, working on the carts. Until I learned where the sharp places were."

Sure enough, Vincent's hands were hard and

rough but unmarked by cuts as he tended to Shelby's wound, first cleansing it, then applying some antibacterial lotion and a fresh bandage. She'd recently had a tetanus shot, so it wouldn't be necessary for her to get another one. But Vincent told her to keep an eye on the cut anyway, to notice whether it swelled or reddened, both of which could indicate it was infected.

"Look, you're in one piece, right, kid?" he asked her. "I don't want any trouble over this. I told you to stay away from that part of the course, didn't I? You heard me say it, right?"

He walked toward the bathroom, but instead set the bottle of ointment on top of the file cabinet.

Noah looked at it and winced.

The front of the cabinet drawer flopped down, dangling from its tape hinge, as Noah dashed up to catch it. Vincent watched him fumble to keep it from falling to the floor. Finally, Noah gave up and the drawer front clattered to his feet.

Noah stammered to fill the awful silence. "Wow, will you look at that? You know, I have a cousin who sells used office furniture. If you want, umm, I could get his number."

Vincent looked at Noah, the file cabinet, and quickly around his office. Then he looked at Shelby.

"I don't know what you thought you'd find here," he told her. "But if you don't press charges over your injury"—he looked again at the file cabinet—"I won't press charges either."

"What a total rip-off," said Noah, faking shock. "That was nowhere near a half-hour ride. If I were you, Shelby, I'd go back there right now and demand a rebate on my $7.50."

"Yeah, just what she wants to do—let that lunatic take another crack at her life," said Cindi.

They were stopped in traffic, caught behind a minor fender-bender that had police detouring traffic. Cindi, behind the wheel of her convertible, was eager to get her friends home so she could chill out. But Shelby had other thoughts. As Cindi nudged her car around the accident, Shelby spoke.

"You know, this accident could have been a lot worse. And there's no shoulder on the road here. If this were a bad accident, we could have been caught here for an hour, easily."

Cindi looked at her friend and furrowed her brow. "What are you thinking?" she asked.

"My excuse, when Grandpa asks me where I was so late," Shelby answered her. "We still have one suspect we haven't investigated."

Noah's eyes widened. "Are you out of your mind?" he asked. "You just survived Sicko's Sleigh Ride, and you're ready for more? Besides," Noah went on, "Gerald Vincent is guilty as can be. That go-cart thing was no accident. He deliberately put you into a car that was faster than it should be, and then put you on an unsafe track. I say we call Detective Hineline now."

But Shelby wasn't ready to do that. "We don't know for sure Vincent put me in that dangerous car on purpose."

And I keep remembering what Dr. Taylor said at the gallery that day...

"You won't see me again, until they slam the doors on this place for good and you have to auction off your precious art to save your shirt!"

Dr. Taylor seemed pretty angry.

"But how will you get to question him?" Cindi asked.

Her wily friend looked down at the fresh bandage covering the wound that had stopped bleeding.

"Just drop me off at the end of his driveway," Shelby told them.

Dr. Taylor's house stood far down toward the water, away from the street, at the end of a private, sandy lane. The driveway was unmarked. The house, very close to the shore, was hard to see from the public street, because the lower floor was below street level and plantings near the road obscured the upper story.

It was getting dark as Shelby walked down the driveway to the house, pretending to limp from some imaginary accident that caused the trickle of blood dribbling down her leg. Ripping the bandage off the wound had hurt like crazy, since it reopened the cut. Driving away to wait for Shelby at a nearby Mexican restaurant, there were tears in Cindi's eyes from thinking about what Shelby, her friend, was putting herself through to help her Uncle Phil.

The driveway curved to the right, under a covered car park. Shelby looked up at the house in front of her. It was built more recently than her grandfather's, and although it was smaller than the bed-and-breakfast, it looked like an expensive home.

Her footsteps on the gravel driveway were the only sound she heard until she got very close to the house. Then she heard the waves crashing against the rocks. Walking around to the water side of the house, Shelby saw a small launch tied to the doctor's dock. His neighbor never saw his car leave the night of the robbery, she remembered the detective saying. But here was a way he could have gone out to commit the crime.

The water was so vast and the house so remote. Thank goodness she came with Cindi and Noah. Otherwise, if something happened to her here, no one would ever know.

Back in front of the house, Shelby rang the bell. Through a small window next to the door, she could see Dr. Taylor's back at what she correctly guessed was his dining room table. At the bed-and-breakfast, they were used to having unexpected guests arrive at strange hours, but she could tell the bell startled Dr. Taylor.

He turned to peer over his shoulder at the

door. She smiled and waved back at him. Puzzled, the doctor came to the door to admit her.

"I was riding my bike and fell, just outside your house," Shelby said. "I'm really sorry to bother you, but if I could just wash it off, or get a bandage or something, I think I could ride home okay."

Taylor looked into her eyes, then down at the girl's leg. The wound appeared superficial. "Well, young lady, in a strange way, you're in luck—I'm a doctor," he told her.

"A doctor? Imagine that!" Shelby said.

"Yes—and even though you don't have as many legs as the patients I usually see, I think we might have something to patch you up," he said, stepping away from the door to allow her entry.

"Oh—you're a veterinarian," Shelby said, as though the idea was new to her.

"Dr. Taylor," he replied, smiling broadly. *Those teeth,* Shelby thought. *He looks like some kind of wild animal himself.*

Shelby took a few steps through the hallway, looking around her at the walls. She let out a low whistle. Everywhere she looked were paintings. Some were quite famous. She didn't know the names of all the artists, but she recognized the works from books she had seen and from films they showed at school.

"Wow, this is some collection," she said, her eyes roving from canvas to canvas. She looked back and saw Taylor watching her, seeming to enjoy his collection even more while having it admired by someone else.

The doctor stepped in front of her and disappeared into a small bathroom. The door closed only part-way behind him.

"Just give me a moment to wash up," he said as the sink ran. "Then we'll have a look, Miss—?"

Shelby decided not to lie. If he was innocent of the crime, there was no danger in revealing her identity to him. If his was the threatening voice on the phone, he probably knew who she was anyway.

"Shelby Woo," she told him. She watched the doctor's back as she said her name, looking for some reaction. But he just went on with his scrubbing. For a moment, she wasn't even certain he heard her. At last, he turned off the water. He dried his hands on the towel hanging behind the door, then turned to reach into a dispenser box of disposable latex gloves.

When he came out of the bathroom, he was stretching his fingers to get the gloves tight. "Well, Shelby, let's clean up that bruise of yours," he told her, pulling a chair away from the table so she could sit in it.

From a sideboard next to the table, Dr. Taylor brought out the items he needed to disinfect and cover the cut. He spoke gently as he tended to her. "A rather remote area to be biking so late, isn't it?" he asked her.

"I guess that's why I like it," Shelby answered. There really was no good reason for her being there, other than to look into his business.

"On a dark road like this, I should think you'd be in some danger of a car not seeing you, and be risking severe injury," he said. "Is that what happened? Were you run off the road by a car?"

"Nope. No cars. Just wasn't looking," she told him. "That's a problem I have. I guess I'm not all that observant." At least that's what she wanted him to believe as her eyes scanned the room. She didn't expect to learn very much just by looking around the place. But there was some information she hoped to gain by carefully questioning him. Could she do it without being too obvious?

"I guess you're right about it being dangerous, what with that accident out here," Shelby said, nodding toward the street.

Taylor didn't look up from his work. "Accident?" he asked. "When, tonight?"

"No, no," she said, pretending to be having trouble remembering, when in fact, she was making up the entire story. "A few nights ago. Maybe you were out or something."

The doctor was concentrating on the wound. "Oh, once I'm home at night, that gate never reopens until morning, so I seriously doubt it," he told the girl.

Shelby knew she might be taking a big risk. But the auction was just days away. And she had to know.

"Wait, wait, I remember now. Something else big happened that night. It was the night my girlfriend Cindi's picture got stolen from her uncle's gallery," Shelby blurted out. "I bet you know the place, what with your interest in art and all. The Horizon Art Center? I remember because she called me the next day and told me about it, and I told her about the accident I saw.

115

"A car and a minivan," she went on, trying to take the attention away from her daring mention of the gallery burglary. She wanted it to just hang there a moment, to see how he would react.

Dr. Taylor reached around to a drawer in the sideboard and pulled it open. His gloved hand came back with something that scared the life out of Shelby.

Long and shiny, the scalpel glinted under the dining room chandelier.

Shelby had never seen one in real life—only in the movies. But she knew what their intended purpose was. And that they were razor-sharp.

It was no use begging him not to kill her. She had been too obvious. He was the thief. He knew she knew it. And now he was going to dispose of her.

She never told him about Cindi and Noah, just down the road at the restaurant. If she didn't show up, at least they'd be able to tell the police where to start looking for the body.

Shelby swallowed hard, wondering where he'd jab the instrument into her. Would he go for the throat? The heart? She only hoped that he'd do it quickly.

"You're going to do that right here in your

dining room?" she murmured quietly, hoping her pitiful tone would encourage him to reconsider. "That's—that's going to make a pretty big mess."

The doctor paused a moment. Then, as she watched the hand move swiftly toward her, she clamped her eyes shut and gasped what she imagined would be her last gasp.

The tearing sound she heard didn't sound like the sweatshirt over her heart. And she didn't feel any sharp pain indicating he'd pierced her body. So she opened her eyes. Her eyes followed the scalpel cutting through the adhesive tape the doctor was using to hold the bandage over her scrape.

"Nice and neat, no mess at all," Taylor said. "You want to see a mess, you should see the floor of my office. Usually, I have to shave a little fur off my patients before I can treat their cuts."

Shelby breathed again, happy she was still alive.

"I was in that gallery, I remember, the very day after that burglary," the doctor recalled, looking directly into Shelby's eyes. "The owner and I talked about the crime. So, I have a pretty clear recollection of the previous night."

The doctor paused a minute, then continued. "I would remember something so vivid as the accident you describe, because I was home all night. Perhaps you were biking along some other road that night, and confused your route then with another excursion?"

Shelby tried to read his tone of voice, which had grown very quiet and as pointed as the tip of his scalpel. She couldn't tell exactly what was behind it, but she knew he intended it as a sign there would be no more discussion after his comments.

"You know—I just remembered. You're absolutely right, I was biking around the lake that night," Shelby said. "That's where the accident happened. My mistake."

At first, she had hoped to get some reaction from Dr. Taylor that would incriminate him. After that, she just hoped to get out of his house alive. *One out of two ain't bad*, Shelby thought as she thanked the doctor and pretended to limp again toward the door.

"Should I check that leg, too?" the doctor asked her.

"What?" Shelby asked.

"When you walked in, you were limping on the other leg," he said, pointing.

Shelby inhaled sharply. How could she make such a stupid mistake?

"Yeah, it feels all better now," she said, trying to cover. "This other one just fell asleep. You know, from sitting. Bad circulation. It runs in my family." She shook her leg, then stepped on it again. "There, I've got it back. Good as new."

He was holding the door open for her. "You be careful, Shelby Woo," he told her, waiting as she walked onto the porch. "On your bike, I mean. You should be very, very careful."

He watched her walk down the stoop and up the driveway until the shrubbery concealed her. Then he stripped off the rubber examination gloves and closed his door.

The lights were still on in the gallery as the kids passed through town. They stopped to visit with Cindi's Uncle Phil a while, talking excitedly about the benefit their friends at school were planning, and how much the gallery meant to everyone. Phil was enthusiastic, and even joked amiably, but Cindi wondered whether it was a mask so she and her friends wouldn't see how bummed he was feeling.

Back in the car, Noah punched the buttons on the car radio, absently looking for some decent music to cover the silence as Cindi drove. Shelby took advantage of the lack of conversation to think some more about the case.

She tried to imagine Cocoa Beach without the gallery and teen center. Did the town really need another frozen yogurt stand? Where would kids get their firsthand exposure to art without the gallery and teen center?

Remembering the events of the past few days, Shelby realized, so much was missing in the case. Aside from three suspects with strong motives, there was very little else she could find to help her solve it.

Maybe that's what I should focus on, Shelby thought. As strange as it seemed, maybe there was more to learn from what was missing than there was from what was found.

Well, there was Cindi's photograph. That was missing, until Will found it in the Dumpster.

But why was Cindi's photograph targeted? A reason for that was missing, too. That was one of the things making it so hard to understand.

Missing, too, was convincing proof that the suspects could have committed the crime. Janis Pine might have stolen the photograph, but could she have pilfered the insurance envelope? Unless Gerald Vincent had an accomplice, he couldn't have driven to the gallery feeling sick, if he *was* truly sick. And Dr. Taylor's neighbor was certain his gate stayed locked all night and his car never left the driveway.

What else was missing?

Shelby tried to picture the gallery in her mind, the day after the burglary, when she happened upon Detective Hineline. Was something different? Had something changed?

Shelby went back to thinking about what was missing. Grandpa was wrong, she realized. You didn't have to wait until something was gone to know its value. The gallery was still here, and she missed it already.

Shelby's grandfather turned her ankle over in his hand, carefully feeling for any deeper injuries than the scrape on her leg.

"Well, there's no swelling," he told her. "A little black and blue, but it doesn't look too bad. You're sure it doesn't hurt when I press here?"

"No, no pain," she told him. "The guy at the go-cart place fixed me up."

"Looks like a pretty professional job to me," he answered, his soft hands touching the bandage. Shelby didn't tell him about the visit to Dr. Taylor. "The guy should become a medic and get out of the go-cart business," Mike said. "Shelby, I don't want you going around that place anymore. It must not be too safe. Who ever heard of getting hurt on a go-cart ride?"

Someone who's been targeted by a prime suspect, that's who, Shelby thought. As her grandfather put her foot back on the floor, she felt against her leg her grandfather's soft but strong fingers, all finished with attending to her bruise. And something odd occurred to her.

Each of her suspects had taken care of her in one way or another. Janis Pine, when she pressed the money into Shelby's hand, had been concerned that she get something to eat. Gerald Vincent had cleaned and bandaged her wound at the track. Dr. Taylor had applied the new dressing after Shelby intentionally reinjured it.

It might have been the first case she ever had where there had been that kind of physical contact with each of the suspects.

Suddenly Shelby realized what wasn't there to see, what was missing in this case. Something at the gallery was missing. Not that first day, or when she returned to look some more. But that very night.

She wasn't sure yet why it was important, but she had to know more facts. She quickly dialed Cindi's number.

"Cindi," she said hurriedly when her friend picked up. "Tonight, at the gallery, where was Amber?"

"Oh, Uncle Phil has the cat at home now," she answered. "That cat went totally bonkers."

"What do you mean?" Shelby asked her.

"Too bad, because she's such a pretty cat. But aside from Uncle Phil, for the past few weeks, she just wants to attack anybody who comes near her," Cindi replied. "She used to let everybody pet her, but Uncle Phil couldn't take the risk anymore."

Shelby reviewed everything in her mind. And finally, it clicked. She had it. The solution!

"Cindi," she said, barely about to control herself, "I've got to get off the phone and call the police. I think I know something Detective Hineline's going to want to hear."

Chapter
11

The little bell on the door rang as Janis Pine entered the Horizon Art Center the next day. Shelby sat alone at the desk and hoped the woman wouldn't recognize her. *Not until this is over*, Shelby thought. *Then I can reveal everything.*

Janis scowled at Shelby. "I got a message Phil Ornette wanted to see me," she said without saying hello.

"Oh, he had to run out, but he'll be back," Shelby told her. "Would you like to look at the exhibit, or maybe at the amateur show, while you're waiting?"

Janis snorted. "I'm not going to wait around

all day for him. Uh-uh, no, ma'am. You can just tell him I'll be next door if he needs me."

The gift-shop owner walked to the door and opened it. She looked back at Shelby. "You seem familiar, but I can't place you," she told the girl.

Shelby recalled the incident with Janis was at night, and that Janis supposedly didn't see well at night. "I like to go to C.J.'s sometimes, for the soup. Maybe that's where you've seen me," Shelby told her.

Janis squinted at Shelby, trying to remember something. But it wouldn't come to her. But the thought of C.J.'s soup seemed to brighten her. "Isn't theirs the best in town? Today is Yankee bean!" she sang out cheerily, obviously looking forward to lunch.

As the door shut behind her, Shelby wished the woman had stayed. The detective hadn't arrived yet and she wanted Janis there when he did. But at least she knew where to find the woman.

A moment later, Shelby could see Gerald Vincent crossing the street. After their meeting at the go-cart track, it really wouldn't do for him to see her at the gallery. As he approached the door she ran around the desk. She hid behind a large column to watch the man place what looked like official papers on the desk.

"Ornette? Ornette? Hello?" he called out.

Leaving an envelope on the desk, he walked out again, crossed the street, and entered a newsstand. *Good, he'll be close,* Shelby reasoned.

Soon after, another visitor arrived. A tall, slender visitor with a thin mustache and broken, twisted teeth, his hands thrust deep into his pockets. If Dr. Taylor was surprised to see her, he didn't reveal it. As he entered the gallery, he looked back out into the street. At this hour, it was quiet and deserted.

"I didn't see your bike parked out there," he said to Shelby. "How's that leg of yours?"

"Just fine, Doctor," she replied. She decided to explain nothing, and let him wonder why she was there.

But the doctor didn't seem to need an explanation. "I was expecting Mr. Ornette," he told her. "I got the most surprising message that he was willing to part with some paintings privately in advance of the auction. It's nice to know people can come to their senses. Is he here?"

Shelby shook her head. "He had to go out. Something about going to get the police."

The doctor's tone never changed. "The police? But I understood they weren't interested in investigating the theft."

"Oh, they weren't," she said, her pulse quickening. "And they won't have to. Because when Phil gets back, someone is going to tell them who stole the photograph."

"I see," the doctor said, calm as ever. "And who might that informant be?"

Shelby could feel her heart beating like it would burst clear through her chest as the doctor removed one hand from his pocket, holding a handkerchief and a small bottle with a clear fluid in it. The veterinarian put the bottle to his lips and used his teeth to pop the top.

"You know, Shelby Woo, you seem a little tired to me. Probably the stress of your accident last night—if it was an accident. This should help you sleep soundly," he said, soaking the handkerchief in the solution.

Shelby inched away from him, toward the back room. "Okay, change of plans," she said. "I won't tell the cops. How would that be?"

Dr. Taylor kept advancing. "I got too eager," he announced. "But I just had to have the Dorot. It would go so well with my collection. You saw the ones on my wall. You should see the others. Even more valuable. They're hung in a private building, on a small island I own, only accessible by boat." His volume dropped noticeably. "Some of them cost me dearly. But then, the people who sold them didn't exactly have the legal right."

So that was it! All this fuss wasn't about the break-in. Dr. Taylor owned stolen paintings—probably the ones Detective Hineline had said the police could never find! The doctor was worried if anyone found out he was behind the break-in, they might find his private collection of stolen paintings!

"I'd like to take you to see those paintings, Shelby," the vet said, approaching ever closer. "Yes, I think that might be a wonderful place to keep you hidden. Just imagine, if you ever revive, the beauty you'll see."

Taylor had come around the other side of the desk. He was moving swiftly toward her.

Shelby's arm felt for the doorway to the back office, covered by its curtain. But she didn't dare turn her back on the doctor.

Still holding the handkerchief outstretched, he lunged.

At that moment, Shelby's hand found the curtain. She grabbed it and gave it a sharp yank.

Dr. Taylor's eyes darted up in fright. Amber, the cat, paws outstretched, seemed to fly through the air, her claws aimed straight for Taylor's face!

Instinctively, the hand in Dr. Taylor's pocket rose to his face to guard against the cat's attack. The cat missed, landing on the desk behind him. But as Detective Hineline and Phil burst through the curtain from the back room, everyone saw the only evidence they would need to connect Dr. Taylor to the burglary: across the back of his hand were Amber's claw marks, marking and indicting him for the break-in.

"Are you all right?" Detective Hineline asked Shelby.

"A little breathless, but no other complaints," she answered. Shelby knew all along the detective and Phil were behind the screen. They had been part of the plan to lure Dr. Taylor to the gallery and expose him.

As the detective held Dr. Taylor by the arm, the doctor asked Shelby to clear up the puzzle. "As far as I can recall, you never saw my hands," Dr. Taylor told her.

That's exactly right. I only saw you twice. And both times, your hands were concealed. The first time was the rainy day after the burglary.

The doctor walked directly over to a canvas. He stood very straight in front of it, with his hands behind his back.

I don't know whether you intended to keep your hands hidden, or if it was just coincidence. But even when you left the gallery angry, I still couldn't see your hands.

Dr. Taylor looked down at Phil's hand, but didn't meet it with his own. Instead, he pushed past the gallery owner and out the door into the sunny Cocoa Beach street.

Just last night, at your home, you wore latex gloves, so again your hands weren't visible. But the difference between you and my other suspects is, I got a real good look at their hands. Like that time I saw Janis behind the gallery at night.

A Slash in the Night

"Oh, now, I'm not worried about a little garbage," Janis said, grabbing Shelby's hands and pressing the bill into them with her own. Shelby looked at the woman's hands. She was struck by their softness and strength. Beautiful hands, strangely unlined for a woman Janis's age, Shelby noted. Hands that communicated something vital and caring.

There wasn't a mark on those hands. I would have noticed. And Gerald Vincent's hands were clean of cuts and bruises, too.

Sure enough, Vincent's hands were hard and rough but unmarked by cuts as he tended to Shelby's wound, first cleansing it, then applying some antibacterial lotion and a fresh bandage.

That's what gave me the clue.

Shelby turned to the detective. "Both Vincent and Ms. Pine are nearby, detective. You can take a look at their hands, and see that I'm right."

Phil looked at the doctor fiercely. "Shelby remembered I kept the mail right next to the Guest Book," he said. "It would have been easy for you to steal the insurance payment, knowing what you must have known about my financial hassles."

"You wanted to ruin the business so you could get your hands on the art at a cheap price," Shelby said. "But you didn't count on Amber," she declared. "When Cindi mentioned Amber had started attacking anyone who came near her, it dawned on me—how does a cat attack?"

"It *scratches*," Phil said, taking up the story. "You're her veterinarian. You probably figured you could pet her while she roamed the gallery at night."

"At least, that's what we had to hope," said Detective Hineline. "Fortunately, you provided us with the evidence we hoped you'd reveal."

Dr. Taylor scoffed at his accusation. "Any cat I treat could have caused those scratches."

"Ordinarily, that might have been true," the detective told him. "But Amber is kind of a special cat." He held out Amber's paw. One whole claw and pad was missing, thanks to the injury that had turned the cat mean.

"Remember why I brought Amber to you?" Phil asked. "She'd gotten caught in the fence she was leaping from, and tore part of her paw clean off. I doubt there's another cat with exactly that claw mark in town."

"It's like a fingerprint," Detective Hineline chimed in. "Not at the scene of the crime, but on the burglar himself. And just as incriminating."

"Careful, detective—you don't want to destroy the evidence," Shelby told him as he snapped handcuffs onto Dr. Taylor's wrists.

One of Detective Hineline's eyebrows arched as a warning to her, but a small smile betrayed the fact that he couldn't help enjoying her delight in solving the crime.

Chapter
12

Anyway, that's about it. Dr. Taylor's in jail now, probably for a good long time. Thanks to the kids at school who cared about keeping the gallery open, we had the biggest benefit event the town has ever seen, and managed to scrape up enough money to pay Phil's rent for the month. Bands played for free, and there were all kinds of games to play. Strangely enough, when Janis Pine found out how all the kids were donating their services, she decided maybe she had misjudged them. She even offered items from her gift shop as prizes.

The gallery's been saved for now. Phil's not

completely out of the woods yet, but at least he didn't have to auction off the art.

And I have to tell you what's happening with the picture Cindi took—you know, the one that started this all? It's still crumpled, torn and dirty, but her uncle plans to give it a permanent spot in the gallery.

See, since the picture was at the center of an important case, it's become quite famous. Maybe even priceless. One thing's for sure. No matter what happens to the gallery, it's never going to be for sale.

Wow! I just remembered! The photo!

Detective Hineline planned to show it tonight when he gave the speech about security. I have the photo here in a file—

In the same spot where I put his speech!

I just heard the detective's car horn outside. It sounds just as impatient as he does sometimes.

About the Author

ALAN GOODMAN is the creator and executive producer of *The Mystery Files of Shelby Woo*, the TV series on the Nickelodeon channel. He worked as a newspaper reporter, a music critic, and an advertising copywriter and creative director before turning to television, where he began his career as one of the original developers of MTV. Later, he participated in the re-launch of Nickelodeon and started making shows for the network. As a writer and producer, his credits for the channel include co-developing and writing *Hey Dude*, Nick's first sitcom, and serving as head writer and co-producer for *Clarissa Explains It All*. He also has written and produced comedy and variety shows for CBS, Cinemax, Showtime, PBS, and other networks. Alan lives in New York with his wife, son, and daughter.